An Almost Perfect Christmas

DONNA FASANO

Other Books by Donna Fasano

Reclaim My Heart
The Merry-Go-Round
Where's Stanley?
Her Fake Romance
The Single Daddy Club Series, 3 books
Nanny and the Professor
Take Me, I'm Yours
His Wife for a While
An Accidental Family
and others

ONE

So many people gathered in the staff room, it was standing room only. Christy Cooper wondered what the meeting was all about. The nurses and other staff members continued filing in and she was forced, inch by inch, further into a back corner. This was her own fault. The over-abundance of conscientiousness she'd inherited from some crazy, overly-selfless person in her family tree always pushed her to arrive early to any and every event. Although it's true that this trait caused her to never have to fight for a parking space at the mall, it also all-too-often had her standing outside of locked doors, waiting for the stores to open.

As more and more staffers arrived, it was abundantly clear that this was no ordinary shift-change meeting.

The low buzz of dozens of conversations hummed in the air and made the compact space feel even tighter.

"What's going on?" Fresh out of nursing school, Bridget had tomato red hair that was cut in a bob, and her thick glasses magnified her pretty brown eyes, making her look as if she were in a perpetual state of surprise.

"I don't know," Christy told her, her back finally coming into contact with the wall. She splayed her palm lightly on the back of the woman in front of her in the hopes of keeping a little breathing room.

"Sorry," the woman whispered over her shoulder.

"I can't see a thing." Bridget craned her neck and stood on tiptoe. "This is ridiculous." She stepped onto a chair that had been shoved back against the wall. "There, that's better."

Christy grinned. "For you, maybe. Just let me know what's going on, would you?"

"Sure thing." Bridget put her hand on Christy's shoulder for balance. "I hope this isn't about a change in the Christmas schedule. You're still working my hours, right?"

Christy nodded. "Don't worry. I got you covered." As well as a couple other part-timers, she thought, but she didn't bother mentioning that.

No one wanted to work on Christmas, but there were still patients that needed care. And she didn't have a truly pressing need to be at home on any given day, least of all on Christmas—one of the big days of the year that did nothing but stir up sad and painful memories. So she chose to keep her mind busy by offering to work. Of course, her brother was disappointed that she would be missing another holiday dinner, but she would visit him and his family on her first day off next week. She smiled to herself, knowing her nephews would love the radio controlled monster trucks she'd found for them.

"Abigail just came in," Bridget told her.

All Christy could see was a sea of heads and shoulders. Abigail Bixby was the Head Administrator of Pediatric Oncology. A visit to her office could bring very bad news, such as a reprimand due to a patient complaint or a write up due to mishandling of hospital procedure, or it could bring exceptionally good news, an award of excellence or a commendation of some sort. There was rarely a middle-of-the-road visit with Abigail.

"And Izzie's dad is with her." Bridget's voice lowered as she added, "Aaron Chase could be a freakin' movie star."

Bridget was the kind of person who said whatever was on her mind; the classic no filter between the brain and the mouth. But she only spoke the truth. Aaron was a very handsome man. He was friendly and outgoing, and he always smelled like a cool walk in the forest, woodsy and fresh. No doubt about it, the man was a distraction no matter where he was on the hospital floor. And he was on the floor often whenever his daughter was in treatment.

Christy would have chuckled at Bridget's all-too-true observation about the man, but as soon as she heard his name, she frowned. Isabelle Chase was once again a patient in the pediatric oncology unit. As a standard practice, the nurses rotated areas so that none of them became too attached to any one patient. Christy was working at the far end of the hall this week, so Izzie wasn't one of her patients. But she'd cared for the eight-year-old in the past, and she'd no doubt care for her again since Izzie probably wouldn't be going home any time soon.

"Okay, people, please settle down." Abigail Bixby's voice resonated to all four corners of the room. "The sooner we get things started, the sooner everyone can get back to work. All of you know Mr. Chase, I'm sure. He has a request he'd like to make. I'd like to help him out if we can, so please listen up."

Bridget leaned over and whispered to Christy, "I wonder what he wants. Oh, gosh, I hope I don't have to work on Christmas. I already bought my plane tickets."

Christy just shook her head, hoping the index finger she pressed against her lips would quiet Bridget.

"Hello, everyone," Aaron Chase began.

Someone on the other side of room called out, "Can't hear in the back."

"I'm sorry," Aaron said louder. "I want to thank all of you for coming today."

Bridget whispered, "As if we had any choice."

Christy elbowed her in the leg. "Hush."

"All of you probably already know," Aaron said, "that my daughter's not doing well. The doctors have tried everything, but Izzie's cancer is just too aggressive."

Christy let her eyes roll shut as compassion swelled inside her. That poor man.

The room went totally silent. She heard Aaron clear his throat, then he sighed.

"Izzie has asked me if..."

The second little cough that issued from him was evidence that his emotions were making it difficult for him to speak.

"She asked for a family Christmas," he said. "You see, we—Izzie and me and her mom—used to spend Christmas at our beach cottage on Maryland's eastern shore. Ocean City. My wife is... I'd like to ask... I, um... I need a... Izzie would like..."

Aaron huffed out a breath and then went quiet. Christy could almost feel his frustration all the way in the back of the room where she was imprisoned.

When he spoke again, his voice was stronger. "My wife died two and half years ago. Izzie wants me to find a stand in. For Christmas. For a... a family Christmas."

A final family Christmas. He might not have said the word *final*, but that's what he'd meant.

"I'm sure all of you know that Izzie is a list-maker," he told them. "Let me read her wish list. A tree with lights. Christmas carols. A picture with Santa. Lots of cookies. Presents. Snow. My daddy. A make-believe mommy. A Perfect Christmas."

One of the nurses in the crowded room sniffed and then blew her nose into a tissue. Christy pressed her fingers against the achy lump that had risen in her throat.

"I need Izzie's make-believe mommy," Aaron said. "I need a woman who would be willing to come to our beach cottage in Ocean City and help me give Izzie the perfect Christmas she's wishing for. All I'm asking for is three days. Christmas Eve, which is tomorrow. Christmas Day. And the day after Christmas. We'll return on the evening of the third day."

No one stirred.

"I know this is an odd request," Aaron said, "but I promise we'll do everything we can to keep a festive atmosphere. It won't be awkward. Not in the least. It will be a happy time. I'm determined to make that happen."

Christy could tell, as everyone else could too, that he wasn't quite sure he was telling the truth.

Finally someone said, "I wish I could help you, Mr. Chase, but I already have a house full of company."

Several other people offered excuses.

Christy caught Bridget's gaze, a question in her eyes. Bridget shook her head vehemently. Christy mouthed *It's Izzie.*

Both of them knew just how ill the child was.

Christy raised her hand and said, "I can go."

"Who said that?" Aaron asked. "Who

said they could go?"

Bridget looked crestfallen, but she motioned Christy up onto the chair with her.

From this vantage point, Christy could see that Aaron's handsome face sported red-rimmed eyes and a tense jaw. He looked like he hadn't slept in days. He was clutching Izzie's journal to his chest. His little girl really was an avid list-maker, Christy knew. Izzie drew pictures in that book and kept notes about what she was doing and how she was feeling. On the front cover, she'd printed "Izzie's Journey" and she carried the book with her everywhere. If her father had the journal in his possession, it meant that Izzie must surely be busy with some sort of medical test or she was taking a nap.

"I did," Christy confessed. "I can go. But we have a problem because I'm supposed to work on Christmas Eve. And I'm scheduled for a double shift on Christmas Day."

This was Abigail's cue to take care of business. "Okay, people, we need some volunteers. Who can take some hours?"

"Some of those hours are mine, but I

can't work on Christmas," Bridget lamented. "I'm flying to Florida tonight. I haven't seen my fiancé for over four months."

Suddenly it was raining excuses, everything from, "My parents are flying in," to "My sons are coming home," to "I have reservations for a week at Disney."

"Okay, hold it!" Abigail's voice cut through the throng. "All of us have to sacrifice if we're going to help Mr. Chase. Izzie should have the Christmas *of her dreams*, people. Who's willing to take half a shift? I don't normally schedule half-shifts because they turn my life into a nightmare. So come on, now. If I'm willing to bend the rules, you can certainly do your part. Who's willing to take a few hours? Let's get the holiday schedule filled up."

Slowly but surely, volunteers were found to cover all the hours Christy had been scheduled to work. It took about ten minutes to take down all the names and double check the hours, but soon the room was empty, except for Abigail, Aaron, and Christy.

Aaron said, "Abigail, thank you very

much for helping me." Then he turned his gaze to Christy. He just offered her a relieved smile and grabbed her up in a bear hug.

"Thanks," he whispered in her ear. "I'll be forever grateful."

The scent of his cologne swirled around her, and she felt heat emanating from his rock hard body.

"I'm happy to do it," Christy told him. His dark eyes glistened with gratitude and she repeated, "I am happy to do it."

Because she truly was.

Although she'd never admitted it to anyone, she wished beyond measure that she had been able to make her own little girl's last wish come true.

TWO

Eight-year-old Izzie Chase had big, dark eyes, made to look even larger due to the fact the recent series of chemo treatments she'd endured had caused her to lose every strand of her long, black hair. Even her eyebrows had fallen out. Her skin was smooth as fresh cream; her wide mouth and tiny nose giving her the look of some sort of magical forest fairy who might spout wings at any moment and fly away. The flowered elastic band she wore around her bald head sported a tuft of glittery tulle. The headbands were made by a group of dedicated volunteers at the hospital and distributed to the cancer patients free of charge. Although leukemia was slowly sapping the life out of her, Izzie smiled often, her upbeat personality making it impossible for her to do anything else. The child was a favorite among the nurses because, rather than constantly complaining about her condition, little Izzie was always going out of her way to lift the spirits of the other children on the ward.

But now, having exchanged her hospital gown for black corduroys and a pretty red sweater, she looked almost like any other healthy eight-year-old, save the lack of hair and the shadowy circles beneath her eyes. She snuggled on the sofa in front of a fire with several stuffed animals strategically placed around her and her ever-present journal while the adults unpacked the car and stowed the luggage in the bedrooms.

Christy kept up a constant chatter with Izzie each time she breezed through the living room. Every nurse who wanted to remain sane tried to keep an emotional distance from patients, especially when it came to kids with cancer since the odds were so often stacked against them, but Christy found it difficult, if not impossible, not to lose her heart to the children she tended. She had entered the profession because she *cared*... about her patients' health, physical and mental, and also their overall well-being. Not everyone had a long and healthy life written into their future, but each person deserved to live as happily and as comfortably as possible. And children—sick kids, especially—seemed to have a sixth sense when it came to deciding if the people around them were being open and honest, and if they were worthy of trust. Above all else, they wanted candor and if they thought they were being duped with lies and false promises, they usually planted their feet, squared their shoulders, and insisted on the truth. So Christy had decided early on to open her heart and shower these children with the same warmth she'd have given to her own daughter—no matter what emotional toll it might take on her—because that's what they wanted. No, it was what they needed.

The instant Aaron and Christy sat down in the living room, Izzie began making plans.

"We need a tree," she told them. "And we need to pull out the lights and decorations."

"We can make that happen this afternoon," Aaron told his daughter.

"Daddy, I know you packed some food," Izzie said, "but we need ingredients for cookies."

"The slice and bake kind are delicious," he said with a grin.

"Oh, no, no, no. I want to make them from *scrap*." Izzie spoke the final word with firm decisiveness.

"From what?" Aaron asked.

Christy pressed her lips together to keep from smiling.

Izzie shifted on the sofa, sitting cross-legged. "You know, from scrap. With flour and sugar and butter and eggs. And don't forget the chocolate chips."

Aaron's voice softened as he corrected her. "You mean from scratch."

"Oh." She giggled with delight, the sound ringing out and making the adults smile. "I was mistaken, and I didn't even know it. From scratch is what I meant."

"My baking skills are a little rusty," Christy offered. "But I'd love to help with that."

"Dad, remember when Mom burnt the sugar cookies and the whole house filled up with smoke?" Izzie reached out, grabbed hold of her stuffed elephant, then hugged the soft, furry beast to her chest. The animal's name was Ernie, and Izzie reached for him whenever she was tired or nervous or in need of comfort.

"I remember, honey. It was just two Christmases ago, wasn't it? I thought we were going to have to call the fire department." Aaron looked across the room at Christy and she knew he was trying to keep the conversation light when he quipped, "Please don't make the smoke detectors go off."

She smiled. "I'll do my best. We can make chocolate chip cookies. I'll make a list of ingredients we'll need."

Aaron nodded. "We can stop at the grocery store when we go out to pick up a tree."

Then Christy added, "I also have a special cookie recipe I'd like to try, if you don't mind."

Aaron said, "I never say no to a cookie. How about you, Izzie?"

Christy swung her gaze to the sofa and saw that Izzie had rested her head on Ernie, her eyes drooping slowly shut. Without even thinking about it, Christy rose from her chair and crossed the room. She eased Izzie down and stretched out her legs so she'd be more comfortable, then she covered her with the lap blanket that had been draped over the back of the couch.

"I'm not surprised she's out like a light," Aaron said softly. "She chattered in the back seat for the whole two hour drive."

Christy straightened. "She needed a nap."

"How about a cup of coffee?" he asked. "Or tea."

"Tea would be great, thanks." And she followed him into the kitchen.

While he busied himself filling the kettle, she pulled mugs from the cabinet he pointed to.

"The house is beautiful," she told him.

"It's small," he said, flipping off the faucet. "But it's always worked for us." He set the kettle on the burner and turned on the stovetop. "Barb and I considered selling when they started building the condos next door. The developer offered us a lot of money, but we hated the idea that our little beach cottage would become a parking lot. And we enjoyed the beach so much. Izzie's always loved it here. We just decided we had to keep it. My grandfather built the cottage about sixty years ago. It's squat and sturdy; just what you want when you're so close to the ocean. The weather can be harsh. We've been pretty lucky, though. We've lost some shingles a time or two during hurricane seasons, but nothing too drastic."

He reached up and knocked twice on the cherry wood cabinets.

"You're superstitious," Christy observed quietly.

"Actually, I'm not. That's just a silly habit." He slid a glass canister toward him, removed the top, and took out two teabags. "I'm not superstitious, and I don't believe in luck, good or bad. I can't. I mean, I lost my wife. I'm about to lose my daughter very soon." He glanced toward the doorway, then looked back at her. "That kind of luck would make a man want to drive off a cliff. No, I despise the idea that all I'll ever have is bad luck. So I don't believe in any of that stuff."

Those two small knocks on the wood cabinet seemed to belie the proclamation he'd just made. Not knowing how to respond, Christy remained quiet.

"What with the hospital gossip vine," he said, "I guess you already know all about my wife's accident."

"Actually... I don't."

At first, she thought the frown planted between his brows was because he didn't believe she avoided idle hearsay, but then she realized he must be anticipating the painful task of relaying the details of his wife's demise.

"Listen," she automatically offered, "we don't need to talk about this—"

"No, it's okay. They say the more you talk about it, get difficult experiences out into the open, the easier they are to live with." He stopped suddenly. There was no humor in his small, huff of laughter. "Who am I kidding? It seems like it'll never get easier." He leaned his hip against the counter. "Izzie was in the middle of a series of chemo treatments, and my poor, sweet child was *so* sick. Barb and I were taking turns staying with her. I arrived at the hospital to relieve my wife. She was absolutely exhausted. I should have suggested she stay at the hospital and rest for a while. Get something to eat. Take a nap. But... but she said she just wanted to go home. She wanted to take a shower. Get a few hours rest. The next thing I know, I was being paged to the ER. Barb had fallen asleep at the wheel. She'd run off the road. The car had overturned. I have no idea how the EMTs got her out of that mangle of metal. I spent five of the longest days of my life racing from one end of the hospital to the other. The oncology floor and the critical care unit."

Christy reached out to him. She couldn't not. His shoulder was warm beneath her hand, and she scooted closer to him.

"After the second day," he said, his voice barely a whisper, "the doctors told me she was showing no brain activity, but I just couldn't give them permission to..." He swallowed. "I just couldn't. But after five days of watching her there. With all those tubes. And machines." He shook his head. "I had to let her go." He reached up and slid his fingers over the top of Christy's hand and looked directly into her eyes. "I thought it was going to kill me, and I'm not kidding when I say that."

Every ounce of empathy Christy felt was shining in her eyes; she could feel unshed tears burning her eye sockets. What a horrible nightmare this man had lived through.

"Izzie finally improved enough to leave the hospital," he said. "It was damned hard. I was pulled between the joy of having Izzie home and the anguish of getting used to having a family of two. The house was so damned quiet. I never realized how much life Barb brought to our home... to our family."

She tensed her fingers gently on his shoulder.

He heaved a sigh, and immediately the tightness in the air loosened a little. "But losing my wife didn't kill me." He offered her a small smile. "Of course, it didn't. I had Izzie to worry about. To take care of. To focus on."

The kettle started to whistle, and Christy turned just enough to switch off the burner, then she swiveled back around to give him her undivided attention.

Aaron pulled her hand from where it rested on his shoulder, but he held onto it. She was aware of the heat of his skin on hers. His gaze traveled to the doorway, and Christy suspected he was thinking about his little girl, and how sick she was, and the grief that lay in store for him. And his lack of a focus once she was gone.

She grasped his hand with both of hers and gave a firm squeeze, hoping to offer him some small amount of comfort, but it seemed so little in the face of the dark and daunting times ahead for him.

Again, he inhaled deeply, and this time when he released it, his shoulders squared and he smiled.

"Thanks for listening to all of that. I'm sorry that I—"

"Oh, no." She cut him off with an emphatic shake of her head. "Don't you dare apologize, Aaron. When I'm taking care of Izzie, it's really good for me to know all I can about what might be worrying her, or why she might be feeling stressed, or what's triggering her sadness. The more information I have, the better able I am to give her what she needs."

Of course, Christy could tend to Izzie's physical needs without being privy to the tragic details of her mother's death. But she hadn't wanted Aaron to feel a moment's regret for having leaned on her.

His eyes glittered when he smiled into her face, then he did the most extraordinary thing. He hugged her.

When he stepped away from her, he said, "We need to pour water over those teabags."

Christy nodded and reached for the kettle.

THREE

Colorful decorations hung from the trees in Northside Park, and the bushes were covered with nets of lighting, although they weren't all that visible in the daytime. Santa waited in a small shed-like "house" where children could visit, tell him about their Christmas wish lists, and have their pictures taken. The attendant understood and was extremely accommodating when Aaron requested that Izzie not have to stand in line with the other children. The chemicals that had been introduced into her bloodstream to suppress the cancer growth also jeopardized her immune system and made her susceptible to even the smallest germs.

After spending some one-on-one time with Santa, Izzie had her picture taken, sweetly accepted a candy cane, and then waved goodbye before joining her dad and Christy who waited outside.

"You looked awfully serious in there while you talked to Santa," Aaron observed.

Izzie nodded. "I tried to make him understand what I wanted." She issued a long-suffering sigh. "He doesn't get things right very often."

Christy smiled as she and Aaron shared a look.

"He's got a lot of children to keep track of," Aaron pointed out.

The little girl just rolled her eyes. "*Daddy*, that's not supposed to matter. He's *magical*." She reached up and touched her chin. "I think maybe he needs to write things down. He should have a pencil and a notebook next to his chair."

Izzie was right at the age when children began questioning their belief in jolly old St. Nick, and it was no wonder; they were old enough to remember what they told Santa they wanted. When you asked for one thing yet found something entirely different under the tree, that would be enough to start anyone's doubts churning.

"He probably *should* take notes." Aaron picked Izzie up set her on his shoulders as they walked toward the parking lot.

They swung by the grocery store, and while Aaron chose a pine tree and tied it to the roof of the car, Christy and Izzie filled the basket until it was burgeoning. Although Christy knew they couldn't possibly eat all of this food, even if they had a full week, Aaron had told her to let Izzie buy whatever took her fancy. There was a fresh turkey and all the trimmings for tomorrow night's dinner, ingredients for making several different kinds of cookies, ice cream, pancake mix, maple syrup, bacon, orange juice. One thing was certain; they wouldn't starve during the three days they were in Ocean City.

Soon they were back at the cottage, the groceries were all put away, and the tree was in its stand awaiting lights and decorations, and Christy and Izzie were up to their elbows in flour, sugar, and eggs as they mixed the dough for their first batch of cookies.

"Sour cream?" Clearly, Izzie doubted Christy's choice of recipes.

"Trust me," Christy told her. "These Southern Sour Cream Cookies will knock your socks off, baby."

"If you say so." The child stirred the sour cream into the dry ingredients while Christy gave the cookie sheets a spritz of no-stick cooking spray.

After setting the temperature so the oven could pre-heat, Aaron searched through the cabinets for the cooling racks.

"So, Christy," Izzie said, "how come you don't have a husband or any kids?"

The question took Christy aback, and for a moment she went still.

"Hey, sweetheart," Aaron chastised his daughter gently, "that question's kind of personal."

Izzie seemed undaunted. "Well, she's here with us. If she was married... if she had kids... she'd be spending Christmas with them, right?" She shrugged. "I just wondered, is all."

Her experience from working with kids every day had taught Christy that they had a knack for pointing out the truth, usually in a blunt, no-nonsense manner, just as Izzie had done. They meant no harm. It was just that they hadn't yet learned about boundaries.

"It's okay," Christy assured Aaron. "I don't mind answering Izzie's question." She paused long enough to moisten her lips. "I was married at one time. And I had a little girl too."

She went quiet for a moment, trying to decide how much to reveal.

"Danielle was her name. The doctors found a tumor in her brain when she was four. They tried everything, but they couldn't stop that tumor from growing."

Izzie's dark eyes grew rounder with each sentence Christy spoke. "She died?"

Pressing her lips together, Christy nodded. Then she said, "Not right away. We got to spend two more years together before she... had to go."

The mixing spoon stood right up straight in the cookie dough when Izzie released her hold on it. She looked at her father, her voice soft as room-temperature butter. "Did you hear that, Daddy? Danielle died."

"I heard it, honey."

Izzie looked at Christy. "And your husband? Did he die too? Like my mommy did?"

Aaron caught Christy eye and she read a deep apology in his gaze. She gave a little shake of her head to let him know it she was okay.

"No," she told Izzie. "He didn't die. He just wasn't... able to stay with us. Sometimes people can't."

"Oh."

Confusion etched the child's forehead as she tried to figure out exactly what Christy meant. More questions were coming, Christy could see it. So could Aaron.

"Listen," he said, his tone boisterous, "we need to get these cookies baked so we can have some lunch and then decorate that tree out there. We have a lot to do if we're going to go for a drive to see the lights. That was on your list, wasn't it?"

"Oh, yes! Daddy, can we go to the

boardwalk? I love to hear the waves while I'm looking at the lights!"

"I guess we can go for a little while," he said, "If you bundle up good."

She gasped with wonder the way only a little girl could. "Do you think it might snow?"

"I don't know, honey," her father said. "The sky does look awfully gray out there."

Winters by the sea were milder than those inland. Yes, the air temperature was chilly during the Christmas season, but it didn't snow very often. But that certainly didn't keep children from hoping.

Christy began spooning cookie dough onto the sheets. Aaron came up behind her and placed his hand on her shoulder and murmured in her ear, "Sorry for that."

She smiled at him, and watched him bend to kiss his daughter on the crown of her head. Oh, how she missed kissing and cuddling with Danielle. No, she mustn't go to that dark place. She had cookies to bake and a tree to decorate. She also had a couple of special gifts to wrap so they'd be ready for morning. Focus on this moment, she told herself. Then focus on the next, and the next. That was the only way to avoid the abyss called grief.

Lunch consisted of simple deli meat and cheese sandwiches, chips, and a dill pickle spear. Then she and Aaron wrestled with four strings of white twinkling lights. Once Izzie flipped the switch and the tree was lit, the three of them hung shiny glass balls on the branches. Aaron lifted his daughter so she could place the star on the very top branch. Christmas music played softly, and Christy witnessed Aaron holding back emotional tears as Izzie stretched out her arms, the shiny aluminum star wobbling to and fro, until she found the perfect position.

This would be the last time he would hold his little girl as she placed the star on top of the Christmas tree. Christy knew what he was thinking and feeling. She'd been there, lived through the same panicky fear, the same helplessness and sadness.

She had experienced so many of those moments with Danielle during the last six months of her life. When parents are first told that their child is suffering from what might turn out to be a terminal illness, it was only natural for them to grasp hope in a strangle hold. Doctors are sometimes wrong. Tests sometimes show erroneous results. Parents were adept at lying to themselves.

But, slowly, reality set in and hope was swallowed up by fear and desperation. That's when every moment became precious. Each activity, special or mundane, offered an opportunity to capture a memory that would later be cherished, deemed more valuable than gold.

A lump rose in Christy's throat, but she swallowed around it, moving to give Aaron a quick hug before patting Izzie's knee.

"It looks beautiful," she told both of them. The strength in her voice surprised her. "We did a great job."

Izzie wiggled out of her dad's arms and raced to the far side of the room to take in their handiwork from a different angle. "It *is* beautiful," she exclaimed. "Mommy always liked white lights on the tree. She said it made the tree look like it was in a snow globe."

"She knew what she was talking about." Christy smiled.

Izzie beamed. "I'll be right back," she said, and then promptly hurried down the hallway toward her bedroom.

"Where's she going?" Aaron asked Christy.

The Chipmunks' rendition of All I Want for Christmas filled the air, and both adults grinned at the silly song.

Christy shook her head. "I don't know what she's after. But I really should start baking the molasses cookies Izzie wanted for tomorrow."

He reached out and stopped her with a light touch on the arm when she started past him.

She looked up at him, a question in her eyes.

"I know this is none of my business," he said softly. "But it's been driving me nuts, and I have to ask. What did you mean earlier about your husband? When you said he wasn't able to stay."

Christy blinked. There had been a time when she'd been so angry with Dave that she wouldn't have been able to talk about her marriage or her divorce without the use of expletives and a furious tone, but time and distance had rubbed all the hard edges off her outrage.

"Dave couldn't cope with Danielle's diagnosis," she said. "He couldn't handle the doctor visits, the hospital stays, the tests. I never would have described him as a weak person—" she shifted her weight from one foot to the other as she tried to formulate some sort of excuse for her ex's behavior "—but you know how tough it is." She shrugged. "Some people can handle it. Some people can't."

Aaron frowned. "You mean..."

"He left us, Aaron." Her mouth went flat. "Oh, at first he tried. I'll give him that. He moved out because he said he couldn't take seeing our daughter so sick every single day. He came to the hospital a time or two. But as Danielle's condition worsened, he just... stopped." Her sigh was resigned. "He stopped calling. Stopped visiting..." Christy didn't know what else to say, so she lifted one shoulder, hoping to convey that there was really nothing left to say.

"What kind of man could leave his family at a time like that?"

It was clear Aaron didn't expect her to answer.

Then he added, "What an ass."

"Yeah, well…" She just let the response trail off.

Aaron didn't need to know that Dave had showed up at Danielle's funeral, marched his sorry self right up to stand beside her, and had accepted every ounce of sympathy he could wring out of friends and family members. Christy thought the ire smoldering inside her through the service would burn her alive. And then he'd had the audacity to suggest he move back home so the two of them could start over. Never in her life had she felt more like punching someone in the face. She hadn't become violent, but she had called him every name she could think of before telling him to leave her home and never contact her again.

Aaron placed one hand on her shoulder and cupped her jaw with the other. "You must have felt so alone."

Christy pinched her top lip between her teeth, the pain keeping her focused on the here and now. She just nodded.

Then Aaron's features twisted with anguish. "Did your little girl know? Was Danielle aware that her father abandoned her? And you?"

"I used every excuse I could think of," Christy told him. "But you know how kids are. They sense so much more than we give them credit for." Then her eyes did well up as she admitted, "When she left me, she was calling for her daddy. He was all she wanted."

Aaron whispered, "*The bastard.*"

A tear trailed down her face and Christy smiled ruefully. "I wasn't able to make Danielle's last wish come true. I couldn't make Dave appear at my baby's bedside. That's what pushed me to offer to come here. So I could help you with Izzie's."

The distress that had him calling her ex detestable names just a second before drained from his handsome face. The emotion that took its place was powerful.

"Christy," he whispered, leaning forward until he was mere inches from her. "You're such a sweetheart. I... I don't know what to say."

Was he going to kiss her? For one crazy

moment, she wished he would. Feeling his lips on hers would certainly be a distraction from the turmoil brought on by dredging up the past.

He'd called her sweetheart. No, he'd said she *was* a sweetheart. Big difference. Huge difference.

But he was looking at her with such... She ran her tongue over her suddenly parched lips as she tried to put a name to the intensity in his expression.

"I'm ready!" Izzie bounded into the room.

Aaron and Christy sprang apart like teens who had been caught doing something naughty. They avoided looking at each other and focused on Izzie instead. She was wearing her coat, buttoned up tight, hood up and tied, and she held two brightly wrapped packages, complete with bows and curly ribbon.

"Are you going somewhere?" her father asked.

"*We* are." Then her smile slipped. "We're going to drive around and look at the lights, aren't we? We're going to the boardwalk, right? You promised. It's nearly dark out."

"Oh," was all Aaron said. "Of course."

Izzie brightened. "These are for under the tree." She held up the gifts. "One for you, daddy. And one for Christy." The skin where her eyebrows should have been rose significantly as she added, "I hope you two remembered to bring some presents. Christmas morning isn't much fun without surprises."

Christy laughed and so did Aaron.

"Don't worry," Christy assured her. "I brought gifts."

"Honey, are you sure you feel up to going out again?" Aaron asked. "You look tired."

"I feel great." Then Izzie added, "*Really.*"

Thinking father and daughter might like some time alone, Christy suggested, "Maybe I should stay here and bake more cookies—"

"No," Izzie said. "I want you to come. Please, Christy?"

The child's pleading tone pulled at Christy's most tender emotions. Without hesitating, she waved her arms, herding them both toward the front door.

"Let's do this!"

FOUR

Being a tourist town, Ocean City was flooded with upwards of a quarter of a million people in the hot summer months. But once winter set in, the town was sparsely populated with fewer than ten thousand year-round local residents. The streets were empty this Christmas Eve save for a car or two. But the ghost-town-like feel only made this adventure more fun.

Aaron drove slowly along Coastal Highway, the main thoroughfare that ran through the full length of the town, as Izzie and Christy searched for signs of colorful lights. The object of this game, Izzie had explained, was to be the first to shout out an alert that a decorated home had been found. Businesses lined the highway which meant the houses were tucked away down the short side streets.

"Snowman!" Izzie called.

The turn signal clicked a steady beat and Aaron turned right.

"Where?" Christy craned her neck, looking east, north, west, and south.

"Look *up*." The little girl giggled with delight.

Sure enough, a fat snowman glowed in the darkness on a condo balcony a couple stories up, a smile frozen on its face, a red mitten lifted in a friendly greeting.

And so it went. They saw one home literally covered—windows, doors, eaves, and roof—in vibrant blue lights. Another property was studded with flashing palm trees and pink flamingoes. Still another had an array of mechanical animals set up in a magical, Christmas wonderland complete with fake snow. Izzie ooo-ed and ah-ed at each display, and Aaron had to admit that some of the elaborate decorations impressed him, as well.

He parked near the boardwalk, cut the engine, and twisted to face his daughter. "Are you sure you're up to walking?"

She only nodded, and shoved her way out of the car.

Aaron looked across the seat at Christy. "Are you ready for this? It's cold out there."

"Gloves, hat, scarf, insulated jacket," she said. "I'm ready."

He paused long enough to shoot her a serious look. "You're being a great sport about all of this, Christy. Being dragged out in the cold on Christmas Eve is going above the call. I do appreciate it."

She smiled at him, and suddenly he couldn't seem to draw a breath. He felt as if he was really seeing her for the first time. He blinked, opened his mouth, and then shut it again. She was a stunningly beautiful woman.

Izzie rapped on his window.

Her voice was muffled as she urged, "Come *on*, Daddy."

The adults exited the car, and as soon as Aaron closed the door, he looked across the roof at Christy. Her blond hair curled softly around her shoulders, and her hands were stuffed into her jacket pockets. She walked up the ramp toward the boardwalk, and Aaron couldn't help but notice how nicely she filled out her jeans with soft, feminine curves.

He felt a yank on his coat. "Daddy, let's go."

"Sure, honey. Sure." Taking his daughter's outstretched hand, he followed after Christy.

This was an odd feeling. He'd known Christy was a flesh and blood woman. He'd realized she had a kind and giving nature; she'd been caring for his daughter at the hospital, on and off, for many months now, and no one would sacrifice their own Christmas for the sake of a child unless that person was very special, indeed. So he had noticed some things about her. And after hearing her story earlier, he also knew that, just like him, she'd experienced tragedy in her life. Learning how she'd lost her daughter had touched his heart to the point that he'd been compelled to comfort her. But why hadn't he noticed just how pretty she was? Or how enticingly her hips swayed when she walked? He guessed it had been because, until this moment, he'd been preoccupied, completely and utterly focused on his goal of getting Izzie to Ocean City for the Christmas celebration she so hoped for.

"Oh, wow, how pretty!"

Aaron had to smile when his daughter shouted out the very words that were racing through his head. Of course, Izzie was describing something totally different.

His little girl released his hand and ran ahead, passing Christy in the process, as she took in all the cheerful holiday lights of the businesses and homes along the boardwalk. Christy slowed her gait until he caught up to her.

"I've never spent Christmas near the ocean," she told him. "The sound of the waves and that salty tang in the air give the season a whole different feel."

"Everyone should spend at least one Christmas near the sea."

She hugged herself and shimmied her shoulders. "That breeze that's so refreshing in the summer, cuts right through you this time of year, though, doesn't it?"

As if it were the most natural thing in the world, he wrapped an arm around her. "We won't be out long. Izzie will be worn out soon."

"Hey, don't you worry about me." She grinned. "I'm tough."

Aaron laughed. "I'm sure you are."

"Dad! Dad!" Izzie shouted. "We're almost to the Lonely Loon. I can see it from here!"

"We're coming as fast as we can," he called back, and the adults hastened their pace. "My daughter is in love with the Lonely Loon. It's a big, ramshackle Victorian and the owner goes all out with the Christmas decorations."

They reached Izzie who had climbed up onto the sea wall and now stood, gazing up at the brightly lit house.

"The Lonely Loon." Izzie's tongue lingered on the Ls. "I love sayin' that."

"It's a B&B," Christy said.

The entire house was outlined in tiny white lights. Strings of vibrant red lights spiraled down the full length of the white porch columns, turning them into fat candy canes. Electronic icicles dripped from the eaves and the motion of the lights made them look as if they were actually melting. The evergreen wreath secured to the front door was huge and welcoming.

"Yeah," Izzie said. "It looks like a huge dollhouse, doesn't it? It's my favorite place on the whole boardwalk."

"You like it even more than the arcades?" her dad asked.

Izzie laughed. "Okay. It's my favorite place on the boardwalk in the *winter* time."

Aaron grinned at Christy and told her, "The arcades are closed this time of year."

"Ah." Christy nodded.

Just then a woman hurried around the corner, her arms filled with colorfully wrapped boxes and fancy gift bags. One of the boxes slipped from her grasp and bounced on the wooden boards.

"I'll get that for you." Christy hurried to pick up the box.

"Thanks," the woman said, a bright smile on her face. "Merry Christmas to you."

"Merry Christmas," Izzie called. "The Lonely Loon is really pretty this year."

"Well, thank you, sugarplum," the

woman said. "I'll be sure to give Heather your compliment. She owns the building. I'm Cathy. I run the Sunshine Grill there." With a jerk of her head, she indicated the restaurant located on the first floor of the B&B.

"I'm Izzie, and we've had breakfast there," Izzie told her. "I ordered the pancakes with strawberry topping. They were good."

Aaron didn't think the woman's smile could get any bigger, but his daughter's compliment made Cathy's face beam. "Well, thank you, Miss Izzie. I appreciate the kind words. Hey, you look like you're half frozen. Why don't you bring your mom and dad inside? I'm sure there's a fire in the hearth and hot apple cider too. And cookies!"

Izzie jumped off the sea wall, grabbed her daddy's hand in one of hers and Christy's hand in the other, and then she looked up at them with pleading eyes. "Please, can we go in? Just for a little while?"

Aaron looked at Christy. "Do you mind?"

"It'll be fun," she told him. "And I'd love

some hot cider."

"Great," Cathy said. "Follow me."

As they traipsed up the steps that led to the front porch, Izzie whispered to him, "She thinks we're a family."

The sheer joy in her tone warmed Aaron's heart, and in his mind's eye, he could easily imagine Izzie checking off another wish fulfilled on the list in her journal.

The scent of cinnamon and apples wafted in the air as Cathy ushered them into the foyer. An old-fashioned ceramic Christmas tree sat on a round table next to a guestbook and a dish filled with red, white, and green candy ribbon.

"There are plenty of hooks for your coats and scarves there on the wall," she instructed. "I'm going to go put these presents under the tree before I drop them all over the floor." She took the box from Christy and smiled her thanks. "Head on into the great room when you're ready."

Christy helped Izzie out of her coat and mittens, and then pulled off her own.

"It's so quaint, isn't it?" she said.

Izzie was trying to take in everything at

once. "Just like a big, ol' dollhouse."

Aaron followed his daughter and Christy into the next room. He knew Izzie would go ga-ga over the vintage silver tinseled Christmas tree. And she didn't disappoint him, practically ignoring everyone in her rush to get closer. Lit from beneath with slowly twirling lights, the tree reflected red, green, blue in a dazzling display.

"It's beautiful," she said.

Aaron swept the room with his gaze and cringed at the tragic expressions of the adults as they looked at his daughter. Their knee-jerk reactions were something he was familiar with, of course. Most people responded to her bald head and delicate appearance with the same startled and sympathetic look. Too bad practice didn't make it any easier for him to witness.

Christy crossed the room and squatted next to Izzie. "I've never seen anything quite as pretty."

Cathy offered him a silent apology and then said, "Everyone, this is my new friend, Izzie. This is her mom and dad, and I invited them in for some apple cider by the fire so they could warm up a bit."

Introductions were made; there was Heather, who owned the Lonely Loon, and Sara, who ran the sweet shop downstairs, and Sara's friend, Greg. And then there was a quiet man who sat in the corner whose name Aaron wasn't able to decipher above all the chatter.

Cups of cider were served from the crock pot that kept it steamy. Aaron sipped, relishing the warm taste of cinnamon and the sweet tang of apples. He looked over at Izzie who was happily munching a wreath-shaped cookie.

They sang carols and told funny tales on each other. Apparently, the three women had been life-long friends who had grown up here in Ocean City. About twenty minutes into the visit, Christy signaled Aaron and pointed at Izzie who had fallen asleep on the sofa.

"Thank you so much for inviting us in," Aaron told Cathy and the others. "But we'd better get Izzic home."

As gently as possible, he and Christy got Izzie bundled up, and with his sleeping daughter cradled in his arms, they said their good-byes.

"God bless you," Heather said, giving Christy a hug.

Cathy and Sara took turns doing the same.

"We'll keep all of you in our thoughts and prayers," Cathy said.

"Happy Christmas to your beautiful family," Sara murmured.

When Aaron and Christy were back on the boardwalk, he could barely breathe around the huge lump of emotion sitting like a fist in the center of his chest.

"They were nice people," Christy said softly.

He nodded. "They thought we were a family." The words came out sounding rusty. "It's what Izzie's been wanting. To be a family again. Thank you for not correcting them when they called you Izzie's mom."

Christy just smiled, and Aaron's heart thudded in his chest. This flood of emotions was almost more than he could bear. Thankfully, she didn't say anything more. She just grasped his forearm and leaned her head on his shoulder as they slowly made their way back to the car.

Just like a family.

FIVE

Christmas morning arrived under a lead gray sky. The presents had been opened and wrapping paper littered the living room which Aaron promised to clean up after his shower. Christy was standing at the stove, waiting to flip the chocolate chip pancakes that Izzie had requested. The smoky scent of bacon filled the air. Izzie was at the sink, her hands covered in soapy water, as she carefully washed the porcelain saucers, cups, and pot that Christy had given her.

"I love my tea set," Izzie said for what must have been the tenth time.

"I'm happy you like it. We'll have a tea party this afternoon." She'd stayed up late last night baking more cookies. Not that cookies were scarce in the house. No, there were plenty. But she'd needed something to fill the time after they'd returned home from the boardwalk. After Aaron had put Izzie into bed, he'd come back to the kitchen to help. Christy couldn't put her finger on it, but she felt that something had changed between them. Their conversation was easier, and they'd even found an occasion or two to laugh, once when the canister slipped out of her grasp and she'd spilled sugar across the counter, and again when she noticed a mound of dough was missing from the cookie sheet and he'd fessed up to popping it into his mouth.

She'd learned a lot about him last night. He owned a franchise of twenty-four hour gyms. In the early years, he'd done a lot of traveling in order to help new licensees find locations and set up their facilities, to attend openings, and troublcshoot problems that arose. But once Izzie had been diagnosed, he'd hired a manager to travel so he could be home where he was needed.

Christy slid the spatula under a pancake and quickly turned it over. "Did Santa bring you everything you asked for?"

Izzie shrugged. "I dunno yet."

"What do you mean? All the gifts have been opened, haven't they?"

Another shrug. "Yeah, but... you never know when a special gift might show up."

Guessing what Izzie had asked for wasn't difficult. Sick children and their parents might know what lay ahead in the future, but that didn't stop them from hoping and praying and wishing. Hard. Christy had been there.

"You know, Izzie, some things are out of Santa's hands."

The child frowned. "You think so? But... he's magical. And if I've learned anything it's that you have to ask. If you don't ask, you won't get what you want. So I asked. Santa knows what I want. Besides what I asked for can't be put under the tree."

Christy slid a pancake onto the stack she'd already cooked, and as she ladled more batter into the pan, she said, "Miracles do happen, honey. And one might happen for you. I'm just saying that you... you know..."

She let the rest of the thought fade into oblivion. There was no need to snuff out Izzie's hope. A quick glance over her shoulder told her that the child's mind was churning.

After several minutes, Christy couldn't take the quiet any longer. "Are you okay?"

"I'm just thinkin' about something, is all." Izzie rinsed a teacup and set it in the dish drainer.

"You want to talk some more?"

For several seconds, Izzie remained silent. Just when Christy decided she wasn't going to confide in her about her thoughts, Izzie asked an unexpected question.

"Do you have any secrets?"

Focusing on flipping the remaining pancakes gave Christy time to digest the question. She lifted a shoulder. "Everyone has a secret or two."

"I have a secret."

Christy turned down the burner on the stove, set the spatula down, and swung around to face Izzie. "Want to tell me?"

"You tell me your secret first."

Laughter bubbled up from Christy's throat. "Now that's a challenge if ever I heard one. Okay, let's see. Hmmm." She lowered her tone. "I don't like my name."

Izzie looked surprised. "But Christy is a pretty name."

"Christy is a nickname. Everyone thinks it's short for Christine, but it's not. My parents named me Christmas." Christy grimaced.

"Were you born on Christmas?" Izzie's gaze widened. "Is today your birthday?"

"No, that's another reason why my name is so silly. I was born in July."

"But that's summer time."

Christy nodded miserably and Izzie giggled. The utter glee on her face made Christy laugh too.

"Okay, your turn," Christy said. "Spill."

Izzie steeled herself with a deep breath. "Promise not to tell?"

"I won't tell if you don't want me to." She probably shouldn't have made such a promise, but it seemed important.

"I'm worried about my daddy." The lightness that had permeated the kitchen just a moment before evaporated. Izzie picked up the kitchen towel that hung on the cabinet knob. "When I...go away, he'll be all alone."

"Honey, your daddy is a very strong man." Christy turned the stove burner off and moved closer to Izzie.

This wasn't the first time she'd had this kind of talk with a child she took care of. More times than not, terminally ill children were more worried about their parents than they were for themselves.

"He'll be sad," Christy said. "Very much so. That's only natural. He loves you very much. But he'll be okay. Honestly, he will."

Although Izzie remained dry-eyed, the magnitude of her agitation showed in the now-tightly-coiled towel she held in her hands.

"What did you do?" Izzie asked. "When Danielle went away. How were you? Did you cry? Were you lonely?"

Christy nodded. "I cried. I cried a lot." She thought about the questions, wanting to give Izzie careful answers that would alleviate her fears. "I kept myself busy. I went back to school. I already had my degree, but I decided to become a registered nurse. And after I accomplished that, I started working. After that, I focused on all the kids at the hospital. And I have friends, and the nurses and doctors at the hospital." She tilted her head to one side. "I have a good life, Izzie. And your father will too."

Izzie's voice lowered to a mere whisper. "I've only seen Daddy cry once. And that was at Mommy's funeral. I don't want him to cry anymore."

Emotion welled in her eyes and fat tears rolled down her creamy cheeks.

Christy got down on her knees and hugged Izzie tightly. "Honey, please don't worry. It's going to be all right."

"Will you watch over my daddy? Will you be his friend?"

Without hesitation, Christy promised, "Of course, I will."

~ ~ ~

Hours later, Christy came into the living room, carrying a tray filled with Izzie's teapot, cups, saucers, and a plate of Christmas cookies. The three of them had just finished watching Miracle on 34th Street and Christy thought a snack was in order.

"How about that tea party we talked about, Izzie?" she said.

Izzie set her dad's iPad on the sofa cushion beside her. "That would be fun."

Aaron, who'd been reading a book, got up to clear off the coffee table. He glanced at the iPad and asked, "What are you looking at there, Izzie?"

"Wedding dresses."

Aaron caught Christy's eye and she offered a little shrug to let him know she was as clueless as he over Izzie's choice of iPad entertainment.

Izzie snatched up a cookie that had red sprinkles on top. "These are pretty, Christy. Are these the sour cookies?"

"Southern Sour Cream Cookies, yes." Christy picked up the pot and poured tea into three cups.

"Mmmm." Izzie smacked her lips. "They're soft and sweet. Not sour at all."

Christy chuckled. "I'm glad you like them."

Aaron picked up the small teacup

between his index finger and thumb. "So... why are you looking at wedding gowns."

Izzie looked at the iPad and then up at her dad. "I've been thinking."

This child has been doing a lot of that today. "About weddings?" Christy asked.

"Yeah, and other stuff," she admitted.

Aaron took two cookies from the plate and sat down in the easy chair. Until this moment, Christy would never have thought that a man could sip tea from a child-sized teacup and retain his masculinity. He was doing a fine job of it.

He caught her pressing her lips together at the sight of him and he gave her a quick wink. Warm tendrils curled in the pit of her belly.

"I wish I had a pony," Izzie said. "I was looking at pictures of horses. They're so pretty. And... and I wish I had a puppy. Did you know there are about a zillion kinds of dogs? And I wish I had a boat. Wouldn't it be fun to ride a boat whenever you want to?" Then her words came a little faster. "I was thinking about weddings 'cause brides are so beautiful. I've never been to a wedding. I've never seen a real bride up close." Then she lifted both shoulders. "Or a groom, either."

Aaron chewed a bite of cookie then swallowed. "So all of this thinking that you're doing... does this mean you're adding to your wish list?"

Christy could almost hear Aaron's thoughts. How do I buy this child of mine a pony? A dog? A boat? A wedding?

"No, not really." Izzie shook her head. "We'd need a farm for a pony. And a puppy would be lonely at home if I have to go to the hospital. And I'm too little to drive a boat."

Relief lightened Aaron's chuckle. "Yes, all those things are true."

Izzie turned her head and stared at the white, lacy gown on the iPad. "But we could have a wedding. It would be pretend, of course. We just need a bride and a groom. A pretty dress. Big and poofy, like Princess Belle would wear. Some flowers. A ring." She gazed across the room at her father, blinking. "We could do it."

Aaron's moment of relief vanished and he looked like a deer caught in headlights. Funny how talk of frilly dresses and flowers and rings did that to a man. Christy decided to save him.

"I'm sure I could find something around here that could serve as your wedding gown. A white sheet, maybe? And I could dress it up with something fancy..." The rest of her sentence trailed as she thought about making a dress.

"I... yeah, I could be the groom." Aaron nodded.

Christy was pleased that he recovered so quickly.

"Ew! Daddy!" Izzie's face squished at the idea. "That would be too weird."

"Oh." He actually looked disappointed.

But Izzie brightened. "But you could be the groom. If Christy was the bride."

Izzie looked to be holding her breath as she awaited Christy response.

Now it was Christy's turn to suffer a momentary bout of muteness. Then she saw Aaron offering her an I'm-game-if-you-are grin. There was nothing else for Christy to do but lift her hands and say, "Okay."

SIX

Although finding items to create her bridal costume had taken longer than she'd expected, Christy thought she was ready for the pretend wedding. At first, she brought each item as she found it to ask Aaron if it was okay to cut it apart and shape it into something new. He'd finally given her carte blanche, and she and Izzie had gone wild. She hadn't played dress-up in years, since the days she and Danielle had donned boas and wide-brimmed hats before strutting around the living room. Christy had forgotten how much fun little girls could be when they were excited about pretty clothes.

After the "dress" was complete, Christy had shooed Izzie out of the bedroom so she could make a veil.

"But you might need my help," Izzie complained.

Christy insisted. "I want you to be surprised by *something*."

"Oh, all right." Then her face brightened. "I'll go work on the ceremony. And a certificate! We need an official paper." And she rushed out the door in search of her art pad and markers. "Hurry up!" Izzie called from the hallway. "It's almost time!"

Chuckling, Christy took the small circle she'd cut from the center of the round, damask tablecloth she'd used as the skirt of her gown. She folded the fabric in little pleats and bobby-pinned it at a jaunty angle on her head. Then she pinned some netting she'd found in the kitchen so it draped over her eyes. Too bad it was red, but it did lend her outfit a more Christmassy feel. There. Almost perfect. It wasn't like the long, traditional veils Izzie had called up on the iPad, but it would do just fine.

She stood, looked in the mirror and smiled at her reflection. The editors of Bride Magazine would be appalled, but she didn't think she looked half bad. She'd dressed up the white t-shirt she'd borrowed from Aaron with some gold tinsel. The overhead light softly glinted off the satiny tablecloth secured around her waist with a cord stolen from the living room curtains, the ornate gold tassel positioned in the center.

"Bride of the year," Christy murmured, then she laughed.

Just then Aaron knocked at her door. "I've made you a bouquet."

She accepted the three poinsettias he'd wrapped together with a leftover piece of ribbon. "Thanks," she told him.

"Izzie's waiting for us," he said. "I have instructions to escort you to the living room when you're ready."

"I'm as ready as I'll ever be."

He smiled. "You look beautiful."

Christy nearly snorted. "Yeah, right."

"Wait. What is that?"

He leaned close enough that she could

smell the fresh scent of his soap, and her heart kicked against her ribs. She imagined burying her nose in the curve of his neck, but immediately blinked away the startling thought. Then he pulled something from her long, blond tresses.

"Is that a piece of onion skin?" he asked.

She nodded. "Probably. Where do you think I found the netting?"

"That's an onion bag?" He laughed right out loud. His dark eyes glittered with humor. "Well, no woman has ever looked as ravishing in an onion bag, I don't mind saying."

Christy flipped her hair over her shoulder. "I'll bet you say that to all your pretend brides."

"No," he assured her, softly. "No, actually, I don't. You're the only pretend bride I've met who was wearing onion netting on her head."

"That just makes me unique."

He nodded, his voice lowering when he said, "That describes you perfectly."

She reached up and placed her fingers on his chest, and her brows shot up when she heard a crinkling sound.

"Your tie." Her mouth spread wide. "It's made of newspaper."

"I don't have any suits here at the cottage," he told her. "I was going to use the comic section, but the black and white newsprint seemed more formal."

"It's perfect." And she honestly thought it was. What could be more fitting for a pretend wedding than an origami tie?

Aaron took her hand and placed it in the crook of his arm. "Shall we go get married?"

Izzie stood by the Christmas tree, and Christy grinned when she saw the child had done a little dressing up of her own. She'd taken the clear beaded garland off the tree and now had it draped around her throat in a multi-layered necklace, and a squat halo of gold tinsel perched on top of her head. Soft music filled the room, the tree sparkled, a fire crackled in the hearth, the scent of pine mingled with the delectable aroma of the turkey roasting in the oven; the setting couldn't have been more cozy.

"Okay," Izzie said, "I'm making this stuff up so I don't know how good it will be."

Her little hands were trembling with excitement.

"It'll be just fine," Aaron assured her.

"We're all together here to celebrate this wedding." Izzie gazed up at them, her expression uncertain, but that didn't stop her. "I'm not official or anything like that, and this isn't a church. We know this is a make-believe wedding, but that doesn't make it not real. It's a real, make-believe wedding."

She offered them a self-conscious grin. "That was the opening. Now for the vows. I think you're supposed to face each other when you say them."

Dutifully, Christy and Aaron turned toward each other.

"Do you, Daddy," Izzie said, "promise to like Christy?" She looked up at her father. "Don't answer yet. There's more questions." Then she ordered, "Look at her, not me."

When his gaze connected with Christy's it was all they could do not to laugh.

"Will you be there for her in good times and in bad times? Will you promise never to get mad and yell at her? Will you be nice and helpful and happy... and be forever kind of friends with her?"

Aaron waited a beat to be sure his daughter was finished. Humor twinkled in his eyes as he said, "I do."

"Do you, Christy, promise to like my daddy? Will you be with him in good times and in bad times? Will you not..." Izzie frowned. "Will you promise not to..." She signed. "I forgot exactly what I said, but will you promise all the stuff that daddy just promised?"

The urge to laugh almost got the best of Christy, but she kept her voice steady as she said, "I do."

"Where's the ring?" Izzi asked.

Aaron and Christy were clearly both caught off-guard. They looked at Izzie, both murmuring apologies.

The child's shoulders rounded. "We have to have a ring. It was on the list." Then she lifted her chin in triumph and tugged the ring from her finger. "Here—" she thrust the ring at her dad "—use this."

When a quick test fitting on Christy's ring failed, Aaron slipped it onto her pinky finger. Christy took a moment to look at the gold Claddagh ring. She didn't have any Irish in her family history, but from what she could recall, the ring was a symbol of friendship and loyalty.

"Now, before I make the big announcement," Izzie said, "I want you to both stop. Don't move. Just stand there and look at each other." Her pause was just long enough for the adults to do as they were bid. "You're both smiling. You're both happy. I want you to think about this place, how pretty everything is, how beautiful Christy is, how handsome Daddy looks, and the smell of the turkey, the sound of the Christmas music... and remember this time. Forever."

The smile on Aaron's face began to slip, and Christy felt thick emotion well. However, Izzie quickly came to their rescue without even realizing it.

"By the power infested in me," Izzie called out loud enough for the neighbor to hear, "I pronounce you bride and groom." Immediately, she nudged them both. "You're supposed to kiss now."

"Izzie," her father said, "You need to work on the romantic bits."

"Huh?"

Almost by instinct it seemed, Aaron tucked a curled finger beneath Christy chin and tilted her face upward. His kiss was warm but chaste, just as a kiss in front of Izzie should be. But that didn't keep Christy from reacting to it. Not in the least. Her heart tripped at a crazy beat and she felt a flush of heat roll throughout her body.

Izzie's applause was infectious, and they both joined in.

"Now there's a party!" When Izzie gave a little joyful jump, her halo slipped down over her ear.

There was nothing else to do but completely surrender to the festive air that Izzie had conjured. They ate and danced and laughed into the night.

SEVEN

Aaron awoke to what he thought was the sound of soft crying. He pushed himself out of bed and went straight to Izzie's room. He found her sleeping soundly, Ernie tucked tightly under her arm. His brows drew together as he closed the bedroom door.

Deep gray shadows arrowed down the hallway and he made his way to Christy's bedroom. He paused only a moment before her ragged breathing urged him to knock.

"Christy?" He opened the door without waiting for her reply. "Are you okay?"

She sat on the edge of the mattress, swiping at her face. Whether it was with a tissue or the backs of her hand, he couldn't really tell in the gloom. Dim moonlight filtered through the filmy curtains and gave the skin of her shoulder and forearms a pearly glow.

"I'm sorry I woke you," she said. "I'm okay. It's nothing."

He eased the door closed behind him so Izzie wouldn't be disturbed by their voices, and he walked to the center of the room.

"It's not nothing," he whispered. "You're crying."

She sighed and sniffed. "I was lying here. I couldn't sleep. I was thinking about how much fun I had today. We laughed so much, me, and you, and Izzie. I haven't had such a wonderful Christmas in years. I... I'm so glad that you—that we've been able to make this a wonderful time for her. Then, out of the blue, I realized that I hadn't, you know, I hadn't thought about Danielle much at all today. I wondered if that was because I'm losing her in some way. That... I don't know. It sounds stupid, I guess. The thought just upset me, is all. I'll be fine."

Aaron moved to the bed and sat down beside her, her bare arm brushing against his caused a tickling sensation to skitter across his skin. He took her hands.

"You're not losing Danielle," he told her. Her anguish was breaking his heart. "You could never lose her, Christy. Never."

She nodded, fresh tears spilling from her eyes.

"I mean it." He gave her fingers a supportive squeeze. "It was my fault you didn't have a chance to think about Danielle. We kept you busy, that's all."

"I know. I know."

The deep breath she took sounded calming, but the tone of her voice told him she still blamed herself and guilt was weighing heavy.

"Christy, it's impossible to forget someone who gave you so much to remember."

Gratitude eased the tension in her beautiful face.

"It's true," he softly insisted. "And you wouldn't need me to remind you of that if you hadn't spent the whole day helping me with Izzie. Opening gifts, making breakfast, cutting a hole in a perfectly good tablecloth, pinning an onion bag on your head."

His impulsive attempt at levity was rewarded with her small smile.

"And dinner was delicious."

"I didn't do it all myself."

"Sure, all of us worked together," he said. "And that was part of the plan. Making this a family holiday for my little girl." He shook his head. "We should have found a way to include Danielle. I should have asked you to tell me a little something about her. You could have shared some Christmas memories with us around the tree."

She looked up into his face, and although he wasn't aware that she'd pulled her hands from his, she was suddenly sliding her fingers along his jaw line until his chin nestled in the palm of her hand.

"You truly are the sweetest man I have ever met."

He watched her dusky lips form the words, and somehow, before she'd even finished her sentence, the deep compassion he'd felt for her agony transformed to a sudden and insistent need.

Sliding his fingers into her hair, he pulled her to him. His kiss was long and lingering, and when he pulled back from her, fear streaked through him like a quick zap of lightning as he wondered how she would react. Would she be appalled by his forwardness?

His anxiety abated as swiftly as it had come when he saw desire light in her clear blue gaze. She kissed his mouth, and when she bent to trail her lips down his neck, the thin strap of her nightgown slipped over her shoulder. Her creamy skin screamed out for his touch. He smoothed the pads of his fingers up her arm, over the curve of her shoulder. Her golden hair brushed against his nose and he inhaled the scent of wildflowers and citrus deep into his lungs. Her skin was soft as satin, hot as embers.

She kissed his lips again, whispered his name against his mouth, and Aaron knew he'd never heard anything as passionate, as arousing in his life. Then she said, "*Please.*"

The desperate urgency in her appeal was more than he could stand.

And then they were on the bed, kissing,

touching, sighing, exploring, and they didn't stop until both of them were panting and fully satiated.

EIGHT

A shaft of sunlight cut across Christy's face and she was forced to squint her way out of sleep. She rolled over onto her back and indulged in a delicious, languid stretch.

She was alone in the bed, but she wasn't surprised. Izzie would have been troubled and confused if she'd come out of her room in the night and discovered her father in Christy's bed. The honest truth was, Christy herself was a little troubled and confused about how the events of last night would change her relationship with Aaron.

They had gotten caught up in the

moment; swept along in some powerful, emotional storm. But she wouldn't have changed a thing about the hour or so that they'd spent in each other's arms. Their initial coming together had been quick, almost torrid, but they'd spent long moments afterward, whispering in the dark, stroking and kissing, until their desire had once again reached a fever pitch.

Afterward, she had lain, cradled against his chest, listening to the pounding of his heart, thrilled to know she was the reason for its thunderous beating. She'd fallen asleep with his body pressed tightly against hers. He must have awoken in the wee hours of the morning and slipped out of her bed.

No, she wouldn't have changed a thing.

Christy had just tossed back the covers and sat up when she heard Aaron call her name. The alarm in his tone sent a jolt of adrenalin shooting through her, and she jumped out of bed and raced toward the door.

He was standing in the hallway, his face drained of color, his dark eyes shadowed by fear.

"Izzie's bleeding," he told her.

"Is she conscious?" Christy instantly shifted into nurse-mode, forcing herself into a sense of calm. She followed him into Izzie's room.

The blood-smeared pillow had been tossed to the floor and Izzie lay, flat on her back, her eyes closed, her cheeks pale as chalk. The blood that crusted her nose was dark which told Christy it wasn't fresh.

"Yes, but she's really lethargic."

"Izzie?" It was just second nature for Christy to lift the child's wrist and check her pulse. It was weak.

The child opened her eyes. "I'm tired." Then she grimaced. "I don't feel so good." She attempted to sit up and promptly heaved down the front of herself.

Aaron's hand clamped down on Christy's shoulder. "Is that blood?" he asked.

Certain that the fear in his voice would frighten Izzie, Christy stood up and faced Aaron.

"I want you to stay calm." As she talked to him, she guided him toward the bedroom door. "It could be just a nosebleed. It could be she swallowed a little blood in her sleep. I'll check her out. I want you to go get dressed. We might need to leave."

"Should I call an ambulance?"

They were in the hallway. "Aaron, go get dressed," she ordered, this time more firmly. "She had a lot of excitement yesterday. This could have been caused by overexertion. Let's just stay calm. I'll know more after I get her cleaned up."

But within the hour, the three of them were in the car and headed north so that Izzie could see her oncologist. Hemorrhaging was a danger during the end-stages of leukemia. The harsh chemicals used in treatment could damage the blood vessels. When Izzie had complained of a headache, Christy felt they should give the doctor a call.

She sat in the back seat, and Izzie was leaning heavily against her. Frequently, Aaron glanced at Christy in the rearview mirror, her heart aching to say something that would ease the anxiety that strained every muscle in his face.

This is nothing, you'll see.

Everything is going to be all right.

But as much as she wanted to assuage his fear, she couldn't bring herself to tell him what she knew would be an outright lie.

Christy became conscious of Izzie's ring on her pinky finger and she reached to remove it. But Izzie placed a firm hand on hers, stilling Christy's efforts.

"But I want to give you back your ring," Christy whispered.

The child shook her head. "Later. I want you to wear it now."

Aaron's voice contained a false brightness as he said, "Izzie, honey, look. It's snowing." He stared at his little girl in the rearview mirror. "And it's only a day late."

"Look, Christy." Izzie's voice was weak. "Snow."

"It's beautiful, sweetheart."

Izzie slid her journal onto Christy's lap. "Would you check that off my list?"

NINE

The shift-change meeting had been utterly routine, and now that she'd finished up her final check on her patients, Christy was ready to go home. The break room door opened with a whoosh. The metal latch on her locker stuck, as usual. She shrugged into her coat, letting her eyes scan the room.

She went still. Something wasn't right. Christy looked around slowly and realized that Izzie's box was gone from where it had been stored on the deep window ledge. She snatched her purse from the hook in the locker and slammed the door shut.

Bridget was the first person she met when she left the break room.

"Did Aaron come in today?" Christy asked.

"Aaron?" Total incomprehension forced Bridget's gaze to narrow.

"I'm sorry. Aaron Chase. Izzie's father. Did he come in today to pick up her things?"

Bridget offered up both palms. "I have no idea. I didn't see him." Then she added, "But I know housekeeping was in there just a while ago. I saw her go in." Wordy as ever, Bridget continued, "I heard that Abigail called the cleaning company and fired a rocket up somebody's butt because the techs have been bypassing all the break rooms. They..."

Without another word, Christy turned and hurried down the hall, past the next nurses' station. As she made her way along the corridor, she absently twirled the ring she still wore on her pinky finger.

The Claddagh. Izzie's ring.

God only knows why she still wore it. While Izzie was so ill, Christy couldn't bring herself to remove it. Her wearing it had seemed so important to the child. Then after Izzie's passing...

Christy shook her head. She just couldn't take it off. It was a connection to precious Izzie, and it helped Christy through those first very dark days. It was also a connection to Aaron who, Christy knew, must be going through hell.

When she reached the break room on the opposite end of the wing, she shoved her way inside, and there in a large trashcan on wheels sat Izzie's box on top of a huge, black bag of garbage. The tech was busy scrubbing the sink, her yellow plastic cleaning bin filled with spray cleaners, disinfectants, brushes, and an extra pair of gloves.

Christy slid the box off the trashcan. "What are you doing?" The question came out much louder than she'd intended, but her anger flared seemingly out of nowhere.

The young woman stopped and turned around. "Beg your pardon?"

"Why did you take this out of the break room?"

Bridget entered the periphery of

Christy's vision, but Christy kept her narrowed gaze locked on the tech who said, "I was just doing my job."

"Don't you know this is somebody's *life* in here?" Sudden fury burned Christy's throat. Her gaze darted to take in all the items in the box. Izzie's journal was there. Ernie the Elephant. Books, children's magazines. Pictures she'd drawn. An array of those pretty elastic bands Izzie wore on her head, as well as a Phillies baseball cap. Pads of paper. A cup of colored pencils. A plastic container of markers.

Tears blurred her vision and she had difficulty getting the words out. "These are precious memories for a little girl's father. You can't just pick up a box and throw it away just because you don't know what's in it."

"I'm sorry," the woman said. "I didn't know."

Bridget put her hand on Christy's arm. "It's okay."

Christy balanced the box on one arm and dashed away a tear. "Bridget, she threw away Izzie's things."

"But you found the box." Bridget gently

steered Christy toward the door. "It's safe."

Bridget was right. Christy took a slow, full inhalation, held it for a second, and then released the tension and alarm that had built up inside her.

She'd been an emotional wreck since returning from Ocean City with Aaron and Izzie. She'd helped them create a near perfect Christmas filled with the simple things that really mattered—sharing time with loved ones and creating memories to treasure. But the idyllic holiday had ended in tragedy.

What Christy had hoped was a simple nose bleed had turned out to be hemorrhaging that ended up weakening Izzie and her already jeopardized immune system. Her condition worsened when she'd contracted pneumonia, and no amount of medical attention could keep her failing organs from eventually shutting down completely. Izzie had slipped away from them before New Year's Day.

The two weeks that had passed since then felt like a day, but it also felt like a lifetime.

"Why don't you take it home?" Bridget

urged. "The box will be safe with you."

"Yeah." She nodded. "Yeah, I think I will."

As Christy drove home, she kept glancing at the box she'd set on the passenger seat beside her. She could take the box to Aaron. His address had been on lots of the paperwork in Izzie's file. It had been printed on the sympathy card that had been passed around for all the doctors and nurses to sign. She knew where Aaron lived; she could drive there right now. But after what he'd said to her at the funeral, she didn't think she could face him.

The services had been jam-packed. Aaron had been surrounded by family and friends and colleagues. Christy had waited in the long reception line with Bridget and several of the other nurses who worked on the floor. When she'd finally reached him, she'd offered her condolences. He'd hugged her tightly and thanked her, over and over, for coming.

His words had been spoken by rote; it was clear he'd greeted so many people that his brain was on auto-pilot, and that was understandable. But his hug had been warm and heartfelt.

He'd looked so tired, so sad.

"If you need *anything*..." she'd begun.

"Christy—" his eyes bored into hers "—I'm so sorry for... I shouldn't... *we* shouldn't have—"

A funeral home staffer had approached Aaron from behind and the two men had conversed quietly, heads bent. Christy had been nudged forward by the people waiting behind her, and she'd allowed the momentum of the throng to carry her along.

She'd actually been relieved that Aaron had been interrupted. Her face and neck had been set afire by the mortification. Bridget and the other nurses had, thankfully, mistaken her reaction for grief. She'd been terribly upset about Izzie, that was true, but Aaron's apology had set her on what felt like a razor's edge that sliced her heart clean in two.

Maybe he'd merely been expressing regret. Maybe he was sorry for having taken his daughter away when she'd been weak. Maybe he'd felt the need to confess to someone who would understand.

No. Christy knew beyond a shadow of a doubt that he was sorry they'd made love.

Oh, who was she kidding? There had been no love-making. They'd had sex.

Two people who had gotten caught up in the moment. Two people who had—

Then it had hit her like a baseball bat to the forehead.

She had gotten caught up in the moment. However, he had come into that room after hearing her crying. He had reached out to her in comfort. He had hugged her, kissed her, touched her in all those pleasurable ways because he felt sorry for her.

He pitied her.

Even now, as she maneuvered through traffic on her way home from work, the idea made her body flush hot with fresh embarrassment.

TEN

For three days, the box mocked her. It sat on the back counter in the kitchen, the spot where junk mail and sales catalogs tended to land. She'd plunked the box down right next to the ceramic bowl she used as the home-base for her car and house keys. The counter was located right inside the kitchen doorway, so she passed it each and every time she went into the room for a cup of coffee, or a meal, or a simple glass of water.

A constant reminder of Aaron.

A constant reminder of the promises

she'd made to Izzie.

What did you do? Izzie had asked. *Did you cry?*

Izzie's heart-wrenching questions rolled through Christy's mind.

Aaron was grieving. Most certainly, he was crying. Although she doubted he would want anyone to know it. Men tended to think displays of sadness or grief somehow demeaned their manhood, so they hid these feelings and did everything they could to show the world a brave face. She'd seen it, time and again, in the parents of the children she cared for at the hospital. But the hearts of daddies were just as vulnerable, just as breakable, as those of mommies.

Were you lonely?

When Christy had lost Danielle, she'd felt lonely. But, moreover, she'd felt completely and utterly *alone.* Yes, there was a difference. At first, friends had flocked around her. But soon—all too soon—reaching out to others had no longer been an option since she could see she was a constant source of pain and suffering to those around her. She saw it in the expressions of her friends, neighbors, and co-workers. Interacting with her brought everyone down.

The grieving process is different for everyone. But statistically parents of deceased children took the longest to sort through the chaotic feelings, the guilt, the anger, the silent but overwhelming this-is-not-fair railings. Going through the steps took forever it seemed, until somewhere down the road, the sense of resignation settled in.

You didn't get over it. You learned to live with it.

Christy knew exactly what Aaron was mired in.

Will you watch over my daddy?

Izzie's sweet, innocent voice plagued her.

Will you be his friend?

The promise to be Aaron's friend sat like a chunk of granite on Christy's shoulders, and in the end, outweighed the embarrassment that had her staying away from the grieving man. And that's why she'd stowed the box back in her car and was driving across town toward Aaron's home in north Wilmington.

And as she rang the bell, she hadn't given a thought to what she would say or what she would do; she only knew she had to begin fulfilling the promises she'd made to little Izzie who had been so worried about her father.

"*Christy.*" Aaron's gaze widened, his lips parting in surprise.

God, he looked awful. The circles under his eyes made him look exhausted.

"I'm sorry it's taken me so long to visit. I brought lunch." She balanced the box on one forearm, a few grocery items in a fabric bag slung over the opposite shoulder. She bustled past him. "I hope you're hungry."

The living room was a mess. A shirt, a jacket, shoes and socks were strewn about the furniture and floor. A messy pile of newspapers and mail sat on the coffee table along with dirty glasses, soda cans, a pizza box.

"Sorry," he murmured. "The cleaning company should be here tomorrow. Or the next. I'm not quite sure. I wasn't expecting company."

"Obviously," Christy teased as she

crossed the room. The goal was to keep things light. "The kitchen through here?"

"Yes." He followed her.

She shoved a second pizza box over to make room on the counter for the groceries. After scanning the kitchen, she found a perfect spot for Izzie's things—a desk area that looked clear and unused. He wouldn't have to touch it until he was ready.

"We've been keeping this box for you at the hospital," she said. "I thought I'd deliver it and save you a trip."

Christy breezed back over to the bag she'd brought and began unloading lettuce, tomatoes, cucumber, and the roasted chicken.

"When's the last time you ate a vegetable?" she asked.

He didn't answer, just stood in the kitchen doorway and watched her work.

The surprising weight of the pizza box had her peeking inside to see the now cold, dried-out pie had been untouched. "Let's make that when's the last time you ate?"

Again, he didn't answer. The white, v-neck t-shirt he wore looked rumpled. His jeans sagged around his waist. The stubble shadowing his jaw looked at least three days old.

Finally, he said, "I order that stuff, but by the time it arrives—" he shrugged "—I'm just not hungry."

Christy nodded as she pulled the head of red lettuce from its plastic bag. "Yeah, I can understand that. But you have to eat, Aaron. Even if it's just a little bit." She glanced at him and saw that he was staring at his bare feet.

"Why don't you go have a shower while I make us lunch?" She put enough firmness into the words to make the question sound more like an order.

He said nothing, only sighed, and then left the kitchen.

She went right to work. She left the veggies and chicken on the counter and loaded the dirty dishes into the dishwasher. Then she pilfered through several cabinets, finally finding what she was looking for in the pantry. She shook out the large trash bag, tucked the disgusting pizza inside, then moved to the living room. Making an efficient, clock-wise circle, she tossed the trash, gathered up the clothes, hung up the jacket, set the shoes in the hall closet, and took the glasses into the kitchen and put them in the dishwasher. She folded the blanket that was on the sofa and fluffed the throw pillows. After tying the trash bag securely, she set it outside the back door. Neither the living room nor the kitchen were in perfect order, but the rooms were in better shape than they had been.

She did one more thing while Aaron was busy upstairs; she slid the Claddagh ring off her finger and tucked it into one corner of the box that contained Izzie's journal and her other things from the hospital. It was probably the coward's way of returning the piece of jewelry, but Christy didn't think Aaron was ready to come face to face with the memories that ring would conjure.

Then she took a deep breath, went to the sink to wash her hands, and moved on to preparing lunch. With the lettuce rinsed, the tomatoes and cucumbers chopped, the chicken pulled off the bone, Christy cleared the kitchen table and was just setting the plates on the placemats when Aaron rejoined her.

His clothes were fresh, his face was clean-shaven, his hair still damp. He looked good. Very good. Christy focused on placing a paper napkin beside each plate.

"You didn't have to do all this," he told her, his guilt almost palpable in the statement. "The cleaning people really are coming this week. Sometime. What day is it, anyway?"

"Tuesday," she told him. Then she bustled him into a chair. "I want you to try to eat a little something, Aaron. You might not realize it, but some nutritious food will make you feel better."

"I feel better already." There was no humor in his chuckle. "I can't even remember if I showered yesterday. The days..."

She smoothed a hand over his shoulder. "They run together. I know."

While they ate the crisp salad and juicy chunks of chicken, Christy kept the conversation as benign as possible. The topics she chose were completely mundane; the impossible procedure change that had been implemented that lasted only two days because it had thrown the entire hospital into near chaos, the new family that had moved into the house across the street from her, the new nurses she'd met and become friends with during a recent mandatory refresher course she'd taken.

He hadn't asked about the box she'd delivered, he hadn't even glanced at it. And that was okay. He might not feel strong enough to handle his daughter's belongings just yet. But there would come a time when he would be desperately grateful that he had them.

"So," she said, the tiny word tentative, "have you started back to work?"

Aaron picked up his glass of water and took a drink. "Not yet. I have facility managers who keep calling meetings. I keep missing them."

Christy speared a slice of cool cucumber. "Well, that just means you're not ready yet." She crunched the crispy vegetable, then she swallowed. "You shouldn't wait too long, though," she told him gently.

He winced visibly, and she remembered feeling the same way when good-intentioned people told her the same thing.

It was good advice then, and it was good advice now, no matter that he had difficulty hearing it.

"I know," he said. "I know. I keep telling myself I need to do it. Just get myself packed and start making the rounds. But..." He shook his head and set his fork down. "It's... difficult."

Instinct had her reaching out to him, sliding her fingers over his forearm. "I know it is. It's damned difficult."

"Everyone keeps telling me it'll get easier." He gave the box on the desk a darting glance; for just a split second, his gaze made contact, and pain registered on his face in the form of a frown. His jaw tensed and he looked into her eyes. "I know they mean well."

Christy tightened her fingers. "They do. They only say it because they want you to feel better. But you and I both know that the hard truth is, it doesn't get easier. There's a hole in your heart that can't be filled. It's just something you have to learn to live with."

He nodded.

"And that's why it's important that you

keep yourself busy," she told him. "Go back to work. Meet with those managers. Immerse yourself in someone else's problems. Help them find some solutions. That's the only way you'll find a bit of respite. Focus on something else."

Aaron picked up his fork and poked at the pieces of succulent chicken. "I know you're right. I do. I'll get on it this week. I'll set up some meetings."

His spine straightened as he absently chewed. "It'll mean a couple of weeks away. I'll have to make some travel arrangements. Airline tickets. Rental cars. Hotel reservations. That kind of thing."

In just the ten to fifteen seconds he'd spent contemplating getting back onto the swing of working, his gaze had cleared a little. Christy knew in her heart this was what he needed.

He talked about the cities he'd visit— Atlanta, Philadelphia, New York, Boston— and the gym owners and managers with whom he'd meet. He ate with more gumption, and soon cleared his plate of food.

"You're right," he finally told her. "I

need to get out of this house. Get back to work."

"It'll be tough." She had to be honest with him, but she was certain she wasn't telling him anything he didn't already know. "But just keep putting one foot in front of the other."

"Keep moving forward," he murmured. Clearly, he'd heard the advice before.

Christy nibbled on her bottom lip as Izzie's innocent question echoed through her head.

Will you watch over my daddy?

"Listen, Aaron," she said. "I'd like for you to call me."

Her request surprised him, that was obvious.

"Y...you know," she stammered softly, "if you want to, that is. If you need to talk, I mean."

Nervous energy had her scrambling in her purse for a pen and a scrap of paper. She scribbled down her number and slid it across the table toward him. "You probably already have my number, but..."

He picked up the jagged-edged paper and studied it.

"No strings attached or anything." She licked her lips and attempted to smile. "Just one friend chatting with another."

"Just one friend chatting with another," he whispered, not taking his eyes off the number she'd written down. Then his dark gaze was on her. "Are you serious? It's really okay if I call?"

His questions took her aback, and for a heartbeat or two, she wasn't able to respond.

"What I mean is," he continued, "that construction paper marriage certificate isn't making you feel, you know, responsible for me, is it?"

Her anxiety flared and the too-close-for-comfort mention of their time in Ocean City caused the chuckle that erupted from her throat to sound a tad panicky. "Well—" she grinned, offering up her palms "—I can't make-believe marry a man and not be there for him when he needs a friend, right?"

For a tense moment, she wasn't certain what hc would say. But then he laughed, and she knew down to her bones that he really was pleased that she made the offer.

ELEVEN

February rumbled across the state, bringing bitter temperatures and leaving everything covered in a thick blanket of snow. But Christy wasn't bothered by the cold. Driving to and from work became an adventure; however, she'd always been a careful driver.

Although Aaron had been traveling for nearly three weeks, he'd taken her offer of phone calls to heart and had called her every night. The topics of their conversations varied widely. She now knew he had a sister in California, and that his parents had retired to Florida. And she'd told him about her sister who was a proud stay-at-home-mom and lived in Chicago with her husband and two boys, her brother and his family who lived in Wilmington, and her quilting-fanatic mother and her golfing-fanatic father who lived in Georgia. He talked about his meals on the road, the memorable ones, anyway. And he always gave her a room update whenever he changed hotels. He always asked about the nurses at the hospital. She knew his meetings were going well and she even recognized the names of the people he worked with when he mentioned them now. Getting back to work had been wonderful for his state of mind.

During the last few days, he'd even begun reminiscing about Izzie without becoming upset, and he had asked her questions about Danielle. During yesterday's call, they had traded baby stories, which had progressed to funny toddler experiences, and both of them had ended up chuckling as they'd tried to one-up each other with new-parent craziness.

When a parent lost a child, it was

almost impossible to find someone who felt comfortable listening to the recounting of precious memories. Such talk made others feel awkward, so grieving parents kept their thoughts to themselves. But it was different between Aaron and Christy. Both of them knew what it was like. Both of them had both had crawled through the horrific trenches of grief and were trying to come out on the other side. Being able to talk about their kids was a relief, and Christy honestly looked forward to hearing the phone ring.

As if her thoughts had conjured the real thing, her cell chirped, and seeing his name in the ID box filled her with happiness.

"Hey," she greeted.

"Hi, ya," he said. "So how was your day?"

"Good. Really good. Bridget's man is coming to town for Valentine's Day, so she's walking on air."

He knew all about Bridget's fiancée who was attending med school in Florida.

"That'll be fun for them," he said.

They discussed dinner; she was planning on having last bit of the leftover vegetable soup she'd made, and he'd enjoyed meatloaf and mashed potatoes cooked to order at a local diner. Then the conversation morphed to discussion on comfort foods.

She found herself laughing at some silly something he said about gravy needing its own food group, and she was struck by how much she thoroughly enjoyed talking with him about a lot of nothing.

"My last meeting is coming up," he told her. "I'll be flying home late Friday night."

"Won't you be tired? Should you wait until Saturday to fly home?"

His soft chuckle rumbled in her ear and sent a shiver coursing across her skin.

"I won't be flying the plane, Christy."

She grinned. "Of course."

"Besides, I'm ready to come home. I've been away long enough. Listen…"

There was a long moment of silence, and as the seconds passed, the pause became more… pointed. Suddenly, that old fear that lived in the pit of Christy's gut sparked to life. What was it he wanted to say? She'd grown complacent during their phone calls lately, hadn't worried about him bringing up subjects that would embarrass her—like the night they'd churned up that feverish passion. The night he'd slept with her out of pity. They hadn't talked about their intimate encounter since Izzie's funeral, and she hoped they never would. He'd apologized once and he had wounded her, bone deep. She didn't need to endure that again.

She pressed the phone to her ear, listening hard. Was he holding his breath? He must have been because he suddenly expelled it audibly.

"I'm going to get off here and jump into the shower. You have a good night, okay?"

"You too."

She disconnected the call and sat staring across the room. The fear slowly subsiding, and then she realized she was filled with... something. Longing? An achy yearning?

What the devil was wrong with her?

She missed him!

When exactly had her days begun revolving around Aaron's nightly phone call? While at work, she made mental notes of things that happened, things that she could share with him. When the phone rang, she had a visceral reaction. His calls brought her such heart-palpitating joy. His voice made her smile. That light laugh of his, the one that rumbled from deep in his chest, could make her toes curl.

If she didn't know better…

"Oh, hell." She uttered the words with a drawn out groan.

She'd reached out to Aaron because she'd promised his daughter that she'd watch over him. Christy had talked herself into visiting him that first time, and she'd resigned herself to being his phone-a-friend.

How on earth had she allowed herself to fall in love with the man?

TWELVE

The phone jarred Christy awake. Her eyes popped open and she sat up straight, automatically reaching for her cell phone on the coffee table.

Aaron's name showed on the screen, and she frowned when she saw the time.

"Hello? Aaron, are you okay?"

"It's not too late, is it?"

"No," she murmured the polite answer even as she rubbed the sleep from her eyes.

"I wasn't going to call tonight," he said. "I got in so late. But I couldn't sleep. Then I..." He heaved a sigh. "I felt this overwhelming need to talk to you. I have something I want to show you. Something you, maybe, can help me figure out? But I obviously woke you."

"Yeah, I fell asleep on the sofa." Waiting for his call, she silently added.

"Ah, that explains why your lights are on."

"You're outside?" She stood and crossed to the living room window.

"I was wide awake and feeling antsy, so I went for a drive," he told her. "I ended up at your place."

The fog of sleep she'd felt just a moment before disappeared completely. "Well, don't sit out there. Come on in."

"You're sure."

"Of course. I'm sure. I'm positive." Christy ended the call with a quick tap on the cell's screen. She finger-combed her hair and smoothed her palm over the front of her satin dressing gown before moving to unlock the front door.

"Hi," he greeted softly.

If the glint in his gaze hadn't alerted her that he was happy to see her, his unexpected hug left no doubt. When he pulled back from her, even he looked surprised.

Heat skittered through Christy like summer lightning and she feared he might sense her body's reaction to him.

"Sorry, but it's really good to see you," he said. "I've missed you."

Nervousness made her laugh. "But we've talked almost every night."

"I know. But—" he shrugged "—talking isn't the same as seeing your beautiful face."

Self-consciousness had her dipping her chin. "Aaron, I washed off all my make-up hours ago." But she'd be lying if she said his compliment didn't please her.

Again, he lifted a shoulder. "I'm just telling the truth."

Then she noticed that he had Izzie's journal in one hand.

"You've sorted through the box," she said.

He nodded. "The house felt so empty when I arrived home. I was missing her, you know? So I decided to look through her journal." He held the book in both hands now. "I... um, I really hate to say this, but I think my little princess set us up?"

Confusion knit Christy's brow. "What are you talking about?"

"Can we sit?" He indicated the sofa.

"Sure," she told him, and followed on his heels as he crossed the room. "Do you want anything? Coffee? A cup of tea?"

"No, thanks." He sat down and waited for her to do the same. "Remember when Izzie talked about wanting a puppy... and a boat?"

Christy sat next to him. "And a pony." She nodded.

"Yeah, and that's when she brought up that regret of hers." He opened the journal and began turning the pages. "About never being a bride... or *seeing* a bride, or attending a wedding. Whatever it was she said exactly."

"I remember," Christy whispered. What she wanted to say was, *I'll never forget*, because she had dwelled on and dreamed about what had followed that night between herself and Aaron ever since.

"Well, Izzie wrote about it in her journal," he told her. He turned a page, then another. "Here. Right here."

The printing was wobbly and there were some spelling mistakes, but Izzie did a great job of describing Christy's home-made bridal gown. Izzie had even called Christy's red onion-bag veil both *"beeyouteaful"* and *"injeanyous."*

Aaron ran his finger to the bottom of the page and read, "'I did it,' she writes here. 'I got them to get married. Now, if only Santa will make my Christmas wish come and make it stick.'"

They looked at each other, and it quickly became apparent that he was waiting for her to respond.

"Well," she began, "she did tell me that what she's asked Santa for hadn't arrived on Christmas. She said she'd asked for a miracle. I thought she'd meant for herself. It's kind of endearing that she asked Santa for—"

"Oh, come on," he cut her off. "It's not endearing. It's devious. She played us like a piano."

The enormity of the offense he felt brought a grin to her face that couldn't be suppressed. "Well, yeah. She set us up. That's clear enough."

"How does a kid learn to be so manipulative?" he asked. "She was eight, for criminy's sake."

Humor had Christy's shoulders shaking. She chewed her top lip, but couldn't keep the chuckle from escaping.

"I contemplated going to the pound and adopting a puppy for her." He shut the journal. "How did I not see through all that? I almost checked the Ocean City phone book to see if there were any fishermen willing to take us out for a boat ride. On Christmas Eve! And all the while, Izzie saw me as a big, ol' Steinway. She was banging on the keys and making me dance. Making *us* dance."

He shook his head then and grinned. Then he laughed with Christy.

"Her intentions were good," she reminded him.

"Yeah," he said softly. "She was a sweetheart. That's for sure."

Aaron gazed at Christy and they shared a poignant moment filled to the brim with memories of Izzie.

Then, as if someone had turned on a light switch, his eyes widened. "Here. This is what I wanted you to see." He flipped to the back of the journal. "On the last page. This is what I've been unable to figure out."

The letters were shaky, as if the hand that held the pen had been weak. Izzie had been quite ill when she'd made the final entry.

Daddy
+
Christmas
Forever

"What do you think it means?" he asked. "Was she hoping I'd be as happy as she was this Christmas? Was she letting me know we fulfilled her wish for a perfect family holiday? Was this her way of wishing me a special type of joy forever? Or was this just some nonsensical thinking caused by all the drugs she was taking at the end?"

Tears sprang to Christy's eyes, burning her eye sockets and making the letters on the page splinter and go out of focus. She fanned her face, trying to keep her emotions in check.

"That's me," she said, but her throat

was so tight the words came out sounding creaky.

Aaron didn't understand what she meant, so she tried again.

"I'm Christmas. We shared secrets. And I told her mine."

His frown only deepened, and she realized she wasn't making good sense.

"*My name*," she stressed. She sniffed and took a deep breath. "Christy is short for Christmas."

Understanding dawned and his mouth formed a silent *oh*. Then he asked, "Your birthday is on Christmas?"

Christy was crying and laughing and rolling her eyes all at the same time. "No." Gosh, if she had a dollar for every time someone made that assumption after learning her given name she'd be a wealthy woman. "I was born in July. My parents thought it would be fun."

He chuckled, then he glanced at the page for a moment.

"Izzie really did want that make-believe marriage to stick, didn't she?"

Christy plucked a tissue from the box and swiped her nose. "Apparently so.

Remember when she said it might be make-believe, but that didn't make it not real?"

Thankfully, he wasn't concerned that she was an emotional mess. People in their predicament simply understood that their harsh experiences tended to cause emotions to hover near the surface; one moment feelings would surge with sharp and stinging rawness, the next they would ebb to something softer, gentler, and the next, well, if one was lucky, humor would strike and send a smile sprouting through the tears.

"You know, I've learned something over these weeks." Aaron set Izzie's journal on the coffee table. "I've realized that, just because I'm sad, doesn't mean I'm unhappy. I ache for my little girl. But I'm always going to miss Izzie, aren't I? Just like you're always going to miss Danielle."

He shifted on the sofa so he was facing her. "But grief doesn't have to be all bad. It's all in how you look at it. It's... it's like a prism. If you set a prism on a table, it's just a hunk of clear glass. But if you pick it up and look at from a different perspective, it can be a beautiful thing that reflects vibrant color. My sadness can be a beautiful expression of my love for my amazing daughter."

Christy nodded, never having heard grief explained in such a glorious fashion.

"I'll never get over losing her, will I?" he asked, a single tear slowly making its way down the side of his face.

She shook her head. "No, you won't. You surely won't."

"How do you think she knew?"

"Knew what?" Dry-eyed now, Christy balled the tissue in her palm.

"That you'd be so good for me."

The smile he offered was small, but she was too surprised by what he'd said to respond.

"You are, you know. I don't know what I'd have done without you. Those phone calls were like a lifeline that kept me connected to my sanity." Very quietly, he added, "Thanks."

There was such intensity in his gaze that it almost became too much for her to bear.

"Hey."

His tone turned light, and she was able

to once again look at him.

"Izzie gave me some advice while we were in Ocean City," he said. "She told me it's important to ask for what you want."

Despite her inner turmoil, a smile pulled at Christy's mouth. "She told me the same thing."

"My little princess was smart."

"Yes, she was."

He shifted on the cushion and cleared his throat. "Okay, so here goes nothing. I want something, Christy."

Her cheek muscles went slack and that made her smile disappear.

"Oh, now don't look at me like that." He reached out and touched her satin-covered knee. "I'm going to ask. And you have every right to say no."

She had no clue where he was going with this.

"I want to talk about... that night."

Dread hit her like a speeding train. "Oh, Aaron. No." She shook her head in small, swift shakes. "I don't think that's a good idea."

"Just hear me out," he argued. "Just give me thirty seconds."

She knew every ounce of dismay she felt was etched in her face at that moment. She didn't want to do this. Not again.

"I realize," he began, "that what happened between us on Christmas night was because you felt sorry for me. The entire trip was saturated with my fear and my sadness and my desperation, and I know that you normally wouldn't have—"

"Wait!" Christy actually held up one hand, palm out, fingers stiff and straight, like a traffic guard stopping cars in the street. "What?" She tilted her head the tiniest fraction. "What did you just say?"

Then, without waiting for him to speak, she barreled ahead. "I thought you had sex with me because *you* felt sorry for *me*." For some odd reason, she felt the need to offer up proof. "You came into my room after hearing me crying. You tried to comfort me... and things just went downhill from there."

"You think things went downhill?"

Frustration had her huffing out a breath. "Aaron, I wasn't describing the actual... act."

Gosh, her mouth was dry as dust.

"The point I was trying to make," she tried again, "was that the—" she searched for a word "—*impetus* behind the act was your compassion for me. Because I was upset."

"Impetus, huh?" His mouth quirked.

"Don't tease me."

"But it's perfect," he said quickly. "That's a great word for this particular conversation. It means moving force, right?" Then he gave her a full-on smirk. "Stimulus."

"Aaron!"

"I'm sorry. I'll be serious." He straightened his spine. "I can't sit here and say that I wasn't feeling badly for you that night. But I can promise you, unequivocally, that I didn't make love to you because I felt sorry for you."

She blanched.

"What? What did I say?"

"You think that's what we did?"

"Well, we might not have been in love, but..." He reached down and took her hand in his. "Christy, I imagined you must have felt self-conscious about what we did. And that's why I apologized. I worried about it.

A lot."

"I didn't feel bad about it until you apologized." She watched his thumb rove back and forth across her knuckles. "It was awful knowing you regretted it."

"I didn't regret it." He tipped up her jaw until their gazes met and held. "Not for a moment."

She searched his face, but she saw no sign of guile. What reason would he have to lie?

Her smile was soft and shy, and that's when she felt a shift in the air. Something warm and delicious wafted around them. Aaron leaned closer, and closer, until his mouth slanted across hers.

His kiss was just as delectable as she remembered—hot and hungry. His tongue grazed her lips and she parted them for him. Hugging her to him, he deepened the kiss.

"I know it might sound crazy," he whispered against her lips. "But I think I love you."

"Oh, Aaron, that makes me happy." She slid onto his lap, kissing his temple, his cheekbone, the corner of his mouth. "I think I love you too."

She dragged herself away from him, then stood up from the sofa and reached out her hand in a loving and passionate invitation.

"You're sure?" he asked.

Christy only smiled in answer.

His fingers slid across her palm, the heat of his skin on hers igniting a fire inside her. They clasped hands, fingers entwined securely, and she led him to her bedroom, knowing with every fiber of her being that this was right and perfect for her, for him. For them.

~ ~ ~

The rich scent of coffee woke her. Christy lay there, a strong sense of wonderment filling her entire being. Was it really possible that her pillow was softer? That the sheets had somehow during the night become more luxurious against her bare skin? Even the sunshine streaming through the window seemed brighter, more vibrant. She didn't think she'd ever experienced a better night's sleep.

"Good morning, gorgeous." Aaron came into the room, carrying two mugs of coffee. "I found some French vanilla creamer in the fridge, so I splashed a little of it into yours. Is that okay?"

"That's purrrr-fect." She sat up and slid back, so she could recline against the headboard.

He kissed her mouth, handed her a mug, and murmured, "I slept like a baby."

She smiled. "So did I." The mattress compressed as he climbed into bed next to her.

Every muscle in her body felt as if it had endured a strenuous physical workout, and after their bout of love-making, she knew there was good reason for it. Yet, she felt relaxed and happy and satisfied. She grinned as she brought the ceramic mug to her lips and sipped.

Stretching out her legs and pointing her toes, she said, "This is delicious. Thank you."

Aaron trailed the backs of his fingers over her forearm. "I've been thinking."

"That can be dangerous."

He chuckled. "We've gone about this all

wrong."

The tiniest frown drew her eyebrows closer together. "Wrong? You think so?"

"Wait," he said. "Let me rephrase. We've gone about this extremely unconventionally."

She offered up a slow nod, even though she still wasn't sure where this conversation was leading.

"What I mean is, we've done things ass-backwards."

His foot slid beneath the covers and came to rest snuggled up against hers.

"We got married." He grinned as he added, "Sort of."

"Sort of," she parroted.

"Hey, I have the official certificate."

She just chuckled.

"We got the sex thing down almost immediately," he said.

The sensuous suggestion in his tone conjured thoughts of his hands and lips on her body which caused heat to suffuse her chest, her neck, and her face.

"Okay," she said, "I'll agree with that."

"And after learning last night that neither of us snores," he told her, "we've learned the sleeping arrangements are great."

"Hold on. Who told you that you don't snore?"

His jaw actually went slack, but the twinkle in her eye quickly told him she was just teasing. His mouth screwed up and his eyes narrowed. She kissed his shoulder in silent apology.

"The sleeping arrangements are near perfect, I'd say," she finally agreed.

He leaned close, until his upper arm made contact with hers, and then he bent his head so that he could whisper in her ear. "Now that we've got all that, you know, piddling stuff out of the way, what do you say we try some honest-to-goodness dating?"

The hope and promise she heard in his voice had love flooding through her. This man understood her. He knew, first hand, of the storms she'd faced. And she could help him weather life's assaults like no one else could. They were good for each other.

And it didn't hurt that he was the sexiest guy she'd ever laid eyes on.

She smiled, striving to express all the

happiness and promise that made her feel as if she were floating six inches above the bed.

"I think dating would be a really good next step."

EPILOGUE

Bucking tradition became their approach to life. Over the past ten months, they discovered that not conforming to the rules brought them much more delight than it should. The mutatis mutandis philosophy they'd adopted offered a sense of conspiratorial joy that both of them reveled in. And to think, Aaron had never considered himself a rebel—until he'd met Christy.

And it was in that very vein that the two of them now stood on the beach, in the dead of winter, with a pastor who was right smack-dab in the middle of performing their wedding ceremony. It was Christmas Eve, and a light snow tumbled from the sky. His beautiful soon-to-be-wife wore a sexy red dress that hugged her luscious curves, and she carried a simple bouquet that she'd put together herself. Where she found peonies this time of year was beyond him. But she'd proven to him over and over again during these past months that she was an amazing and resourceful woman. The circle of red plastic mesh she'd pinned to her hair sassily covered most of her forehead and one eye, and Aaron wanted to laugh right out loud every time the pastor's gaze darted to it. Clearly, the man was trying to decide if that really was an onion bag on the bride's head.

Aaron had chosen to wear shorts and flip-flops, and as the sharp, salty chill stung his skin, he realized he probably should have worn trousers. And a coat would have been wise. However, that would have taken some of the fun out the day, and they wouldn't be outside for more than a few minutes anyway. Soon, they'd race for the cottage and the cozy fire that was just a couple hundred yards away over the sand dune.

As soon as they had stepped out onto the shore, they had worked together to gather up a mound of sand, a tiny, make-shift altar of sorts, in which they had stuck two long-stemmed white roses—one for Danielle, and one for Izzie. Every time Aaron glanced down at the pristine flowers, he smiled and marveled at the fact that the two little girls had, essentially, brought him and Christy together.

Once he and Christy had started dating, they had discovered their many similar tastes. They both loved music, and enjoyed traveling and exploring new places. Both of them harbored a secret love of real-life television crime shows, and they spent many an evening trying to be the first to guess who-done-it. The best thing they had in common, though, would have to be their love of laugher. They'd gone though so much pain in the past that they instinctively looked for reasons to smile.

As the weeks and month went by, their love for each other grew into something deep and abiding. A lasting kind of love. So the next step, they decided, was to take that make-believe marriage certificate Izzie had drawn and turn it into one that met all the criteria of the law, one that would make them a real Mr. and Mrs.

"I nuh... now pronounce you husband and wife," the shivering pastor said. "You... you may k-k-kiss the bride."

Aaron captured Christy's gorgeous face between his hands and kissed her with the promise of an unfailing love that would last for the rest of his life.

"I love you," he told her.

"And I love you." Happiness shined in her sky-blue eyes.

"If you... you don't mind," the pastor stammered. "I'm g-going home. My wife will have dinner waiting. And I hope sh-she has the heat turned up."

"Of course," Christy told him. "Thank you for helping us today."

"Happy Christmas to you!" Aaron called to the man who was now hurrying across the sand.

"Congratulations," the pastor shouted over his shoulder.

Once they were alone on the beach,

Aaron smoothed his hands down his wife's bare arms, noticing the goose-bumps. "You're freezing."

Her smile was huge. "Yeah, I am. It's great!"

He laughed. "My legs are officially icicles."

"Let me see if I can warm you up."

She kissed him then, and a fiery passion sparked deep in the pit of his belly. He loved this woman to distraction, and he would continue to love her for the rest of his days.

When he got down on one knee, her brows arched with surprise.

He pulled Izzie's ring from his pocket and slid it onto his wife's pinky finger, right next to her brand new wedding band.

Christy's smile couldn't have spread any wider. "Oh, Aaron," she breathed. "I love it. Thank you."

"Izzie would be so happy right now." He stood, brushing the cold sand from his knee.

"It was an almost perfect wedding, wasn't it?" she asked, giddiness in her voice. "And I'm all ready for an almost perfect Christmas tomorrow."

Because they'd lost their beloved daughters, Aaron and Christy had resigned themselves to the fact that nothing they experienced, not a single day of their lives, would ever be perfect. Except one thing. One precious thing, they agreed, that was true and utter perfection.

The love they shared for each other.

Everything else would have to remain almost perfect.

She squealed with surprise when he swept her up into his arms and started toward the sand dune.

"Almost perfect will do," he whispered.

~ ~ ~

A NOTE FROM THE AUTHOR

I dedicate this book to every parent who
has lost a child. Tragedy of that magnitude
changes a person's life forever. Nothing is
ever the same. However, love is a powerful
bond, and I truly believe that each time we
embrace a memory of our loved ones who
have passed on, it's like giving them a big,
warm hug. The heart never forgets. And
although we grieve, we must never forget to
continue living, and laughing, and loving.
Because that's what life is all about.

Are you curious about the women who
run the B&B called The Lonely Loon where
Christy, Aaron, and Izzie drank hot apple

cider and sang carols on Christmas Eve? You can read the stories about Sara, Heather, and Cathy in *The Ocean City Boardwalk Series*. I hope you'll look for the books.

Would you like to have the recipes for the cookies Christy and Izzie baked for Christmas? Just turn the page to find four of my favorite Christmas cookie recipes.

If you enjoyed this holiday novella, please consider leaving a review or telling a friend about it. Good reviews and word of mouth recommendations are the best ways for me to find new readers. Thanks so much for your support!

Learn more about me on my blog: DonnaFasano.com. While you're there, you can sign up for my mailing list, so you can be the first to know about news and new releases. I'm on these major social media sites:

Facebook.com/DonnaFasanoAuthor
Twitter.com/DonnaFaz
Pinterest.com/DonnaFaz

Please feel free to contact me. I enjoy hearing from my readers.

All my best,
Donna Fasano

CHRISTMAS COOKIE RECIPES

Spritz Butter Cookies

This recipe was given to me by my mother-in-law, Rose Marie Fasano.

Makes approximately 3 dozen cookies

1 cup butter, unsalted, softened to room temperature
1 1/4 cups 10X sugar (confectioner's sugar)
1/2 tsp salt
2 large egg yolks
1/2 tsp almond extract
1 tsp vanilla extract
2 1/2 cups flour

1.   Preheat oven to 400 degrees.

2.   Sift together the flour and the salt. Set aside.

3.   In a medium bowl, cream the butter and the sugar until light and

fluffy. Stir in the yolks, the almond extract, and the vanilla. Gradually blend in the sifted ingredients.

4. Fill a cookie press with dough. Press cookies, 1 inch apart, onto an ungreased cookie sheets. If desired, decorate with course, colored sugar or sprinkles.

5. Bake 6-8 minutes. These cookies should be pale, not golden brown. Do not over bake.

6. Cookies keep approximately one week in an airtight container.

~ ~ ~

Marvelous Molasses Cookies

This recipe is one of my husband's favorites.

Yields approximately 4 dozen cookies

1 cup dark brown sugar, packed
3/4 cup butter, softened
1/3 cup molasses
1 large egg
2 1/3 cups flour
2 tsp baking soda
1 tsp ground cinnamon
1 tsp ground ginger
1/2 tsp salt
Granulated white sugar (for dipping)

1.   Heat oven to 375 degrees. Grease cookie sheets with a light coating of baking spray.

2. Cream the brown sugar and butter. Add molasses and egg, and beat to incorporate.

3. Stir in the flour, soda, cinnamon, ginger, and salt until thoroughly combined.

4. Form heaping teaspoonfuls of dough into balls. Dip tops in granulated white sugar. Place balls, sugar side up, onto lightly greased cookie sheets and bake until just set, between 10-12 minutes.

5. Cookies will keep approximately one week in airtight container.

~ ~ ~

Southern Sour Cream Cookies

This recipe was given to me by my sister-in-law, Robin Elaine Rakes Montgomery. These delicate and delicious cookies are perfect for any little girl's tea party.

Makes 6 – 7 dozen cookies.

1 1/2 cups granulated sugar
1 1/2 cups vegetable shortening
3 large eggs
3 tsp vanilla
1 1/2 teaspoons baking soda
1 cup sour cream
1 tsp salt
5 cups flour
Colored sugar crystals, optional

1. Preheat oven to 400 degrees. Spray cookie sheets with baking spray.

2. Cream together the sugar and the shortening until light and fluffy. Add eggs, one at a time, and stir thoroughly after each addition. Add vanilla, sour cream, baking soda, and salt. Mix well. Add flour and stir just until flour is incorporated.

3. Drop heaping teaspoons of dough about 2 inches apart onto cookie sheet. Decorate with colored sugar crystals, if desired.

4. Bake for approximately 10 minutes. Cookies should be light in color, not golden brown. These are delicate and delicious cookies that are perfect for any little girl's tea party.

5. Cookies will keep for about a week in an airtight container.

~ ~ ~

Soft and Chewy Chocolate Chip Cookies

This recipe came from my old Betty Crocker Cookbook. I bake a batch or two of these buttery, chocolaty bites every Christmas.

Makes approximately 6 dozen cookies.

1 1/2 cups butter, softened
1 1/4 cups granulatcd sugar
1 1/4 cups light brown sugar, packed
2 tsp vanilla
3 large eggs
4 1/4 cups all-purpose flour
2 tsp baking soda
1 tsp salt
2 – 4 cups semi-sweet chocolate chips

1. Preheat oven 375 degrees. In a large bowl, cream together the butter

and the white and brown sugars until light and fluffy. Beat in the vanilla and the eggs until well blended. Mix in the flour, baking soda, and salt. Stir in chocolate chips.

2. Drop dough by rounded tablespoonfuls two inches apart onto ungreased cookie sheets.

3. Bake 8 – 10 minutes, or until golden brown. Cool for 1 minute, and then remove cookies to a cooling rack. Cookies keep for approximately 1 week in an air-tight container.

Coconut Macaroons

14 ounces sweetened flaked coconut
14 ounce can sweetened condensed milk
1 tsp vanilla extract
2 extra large egg whites, at room temperature
¼ tsp salt

1.   Preheat the oven to 325 degrees F.

2.   Combine the coconut, condensed milk, and vanilla in a large bowl.

3.   Whip the egg whites and salt on high speed in the bowl of an electric mixer fitted with the whisk attachment until they make soft peaks.

4.   Carefully fold the egg whites into the coconut mixture.

5. Drop the batter onto sheet pans lined with parchment paper using either a 1 3/4-inch diameter ice cream scoop, or 2 teaspoons.

6. Bake for 25 to 30 minutes, until golden brown.

7. Cool on wire racks.

~ ~ ~

Peanut Butter Crisscross Cookies

½ cup peanut butter
½ cup vegetable shortening
½ cup white sugar
½ cup brown sugar
1 egg
1 ¼ cups all purpose flour
¾ teaspoon baking soda
½ teaspoon baking powder
¼ teaspoon salt

1. Heat oven to 375°.

2. Mix together the peanut butter, shortening, white sugar, and brown sugar. Add the egg and stir until well incorporated. Add in the dry ingredients.

3. Roll dough into ¾ inch balls and place on cookie sheet 2 inches apart. Press a fork into each cookie,

flattening slightly, to make a crisscross pattern.

4. Bake for approximately 9 minutes. Let cookies cool for a few minutes before removing them from the cookie sheet.

Space to jot down your favorite Christmas cookie recipes:

www.ingramcontent.com/pod-product-compliance
Lightning Source LLC
Chambersburg PA
CBHW050951120626
46552CB00001B/482